THE DARK SIDE
OF DESIRE

BY
JULIA JAMES

MILLS & BOON

First published in Great Britain 2012
by Mills & Boon, an imprint of Harlequin (UK) Limited,
Eton House, 18-24 Paradise Road, Richmond, Surrey TW9 1SR

© Julia James 2012

ISBN: 978 0 263 89077 8

Harlequin (UK) policy is to use papers that are natural, renewable and recyclable products and made from wood grown in sustainable forests. The logging and manufacturing process conform to the legal environmental regulations of the country of origin.

Printed and bound in Spain
by Blackprint CPI, Barcelona

THE DARK SIDE OF DESIRE

CHAPTER ONE

LEON MARANZ lifted a glass of champagne from the server standing just inside the entrance to the large, crowded first floor salon of the exclusive Regent's Park apartment that he'd just been shown into by one of the household staff and surveyed the scene before him. It was the type of social gathering he was very familiar with. A cocktail party in one of London's premier residences, ITS guests, however disparate, unified by one common factor.

Wealth.

A great deal of it.

A casual flick of Leon's opaque eyes could tell him that, simply by seeing the unbroken sea of designer outfits the women were wearing, let alone the glint of precious gems at their throats, ears and wrists. The women uniformly had a look about them of pampered, sleek felines, and the men were also uniformly alike in their projection of self-assurance and self-worth in the eyes of the world.

Leon's mouth tightened infinitesimally. That projection was not always a guarantee of the solidity of the worth behind it. Probingly, his dark eyes lanced through the throng, seeking its target. Alistair Lassiter's back was turned to the entrance of the salon, but Leon recognised him instantly. Recognised, too, what he wanted to see. Probably invisible to the rest of the guests, but not to him: a discernible tension in his stance. For a moment longer he held his gaze. Then, his assessing surveillance done, he lifted his glass of champagne to his mouth. But even as he did so he stilled.

A woman was looking at him.

She was nowhere near Alistair Lassiter, but Leon could see her at the periphery of his vision. Every finely tuned antenna told him she was levelling a stare at him that had an intensity about it that demonstrated she had no idea he was aware of her scrutiny. But Leon had been on the receiving end of female interest for close on two decades—even long before he had made the fortune which he knew, cynically, was high prime attraction for women these days. Far and away more attractive to them than the six-foot frame and strong, saturnine looks that had been his appeal when young and impoverished. Years of enjoying all that beautiful females had to offer meant he knew when a woman was looking at him.

And this one was most definitely looking at him.

He took a mouthful of champagne, turning his head slightly as he did so, to move the woman into the central frame of his vision.

She was in the English style, with a fine-boned face, oval, contoured with a delicate, narrow nose and wide, clear eyes. Her chestnut hair was drawn off her face into a chignon that would have looked severe on any woman less beautiful, just as her indigo raw silk cocktail dress would have looked plain on a woman with a less than perfect body. But this woman's body was indeed perfect: slender waist, gently rounded hips and, Leon could see, despite the modest décolletage, generous breasts. The bracelet sleeves of her cocktail frock showed the length of her forearms, and her elegant hands were cupping a glass of mineral water. The hem of her dress skimmed a little way above knee length, displaying long, slender legs lengthened by high heels.

The total impact was, despite the severity of her style—or perhaps because of it—stunning, making every other woman present appear overdressed and flawed. Leon felt anticipation fizz through him. Against all his expectations, the evening ahead was clearly not going to be only about business after all...

He narrowed his eyes and let his gaze rest on her, acknowledging what she made him feel. The flare of desire...

His gaze swept back up to her face, intercepting her scrutiny, ready to make eye contact and register his interest in her, to start to move towards her.

And immediately the shutters came down over her face.

It was like a mask forming over her features. An icy mask that froze her expression.

Froze him out. Blanked him completely. She was looking straight through him as if he were not there, as if he did not exist...as if he were not even the barest part of her universe.

Abruptly, she moved away, turning her back on him. Emotion spiked through him—one he had not felt for a long, long time. For one more moment his gaze continued to hold. Then he moved purposefully forward into the throng.

Flavia forced a polite smile to her lips, as if paying attention to whatever it was that was being discussed. She had more on her mind than making polite conversation to her father's guests here tonight. A lot more.

She didn't want to be here, in her father's opulent Regent's Park apartment. The hypocrisy of it nauseated her—playing the pampered daughter of a lavishly indulgent millionaire when both she and her father knew that that was bitterly far from the truth.

What did she care for this stupid cocktail party? For standing around looking expensively ornamental in this over-decorated apartment, designed only to impress and show off her father's wealth? It was awash with glass and chrome and the ostentatious, tasteless extravagance of gold fittings and showy furniture, conspicuous statement pieces, and she could never feel anything but a total alien here.

She wanted to be home! Home in the heart of rural Dorset, deep in the countryside. Home in the grey-stoned Georgian house that she loved so much, with its square frontage and sash windows, filled with furniture that had aged with the house where she had grown up, roaming the fields and the woods all around, cycling the narrow hedged lanes, rambling far and wide—but always, always, coming home. Home to the grandparents she'd adored, who had raised her after the tragically early death of her mother, to be enveloped in their loving arms.

But Harford Hall was a world away from her father's glitteringly deluxe apartment and she was *not* free to flee, however much she longed to do so.

She shifted her weight from one unfamiliar high heel to the other, sipping at her mineral water and trying to pay attention to the conversation. She had no idea who the couple speaking to her were, but presumably the husband was some kind of businessman who was useful to her father, for her father, Flavia knew, only ever invited people who could be beneficial to him. That was the way he divided up the population of the world—people he could use, and people he could toss aside. She, his daughter, counted as both.

For most of her life it had been the latter—someone to be tossed aside. Ignored and discarded. The way he'd done her mother. Oh, he'd gone to the trouble of marrying her, once she'd found herself pregnant. But that had only, Flavia now knew, been because her grandparents had gifted him a substantial sum of money. Ostensibly it had been to start their married life together, but in reality, Flavia was grimly aware, it had been a bribe and an inducement to marry their pregnant daughter.

Her father had done well out of her mother financially, and the money he'd got had helped provide the capital he had needed to build his business empire. What he had not needed was a wife and child, and barely six months after Flavia had been born her father had packed them both off back to Dorset and taken up with another woman. A wealthy divorcee, as it happened. She had not lasted long, however. Once she'd provided more investment capital he'd moved on yet again.

It was a pattern he'd continued to repeat as he progressively amassed his business fortune. A cynical light glinted sourly in Flavia's eyes. Although these days the women were getting younger and younger, and her father was the one providing the money they wanted to keep themselves looking alluring for him. Her father had got used to having the best, and his wealth had provided it lavishly.

She glanced around. This Regent's Park apartment was worth at least a few million pounds, given its premier location and the glittering lavishness of its décor. It was only one of his properties, however. There was also a house in Surrey's stockbroker belt, an apartment in Paris in one of the best *arrondissements*, a villa in Marbella's Puerto Banus, and another on the beachfront on Barbados.

Flavia had been to none of them, and wouldn't have wanted to. Nor did she want to be here. But three years ago her now-widowed grandmother had needed a hip replacement operation, and her father had been ruthlessly blunt.

'The old bat can have her operation privately, but the money for it will be a loan—and you'll repay it by turning up when I want you to chat and smile graciously at my guests. Everyone will say how charming and delightful and well-bred you are, and anyone who thought I was too nouveau bloody riche to swallow will think again!'

She'd longed to tell him to get lost, but how could she have done when the National Health Service waiting list had been so long, and her grandmother, not only in severe pain had also been frustrated by her growing incapacity. And her increasing poverty. Harford Hall, the greystone Georgian house Flavia had been brought up in, was a money pit, like all large, old houses, and maintenance and repairs swallowed her widowed grandmother's dwindling income from stocks and shares. There were no spare thousands left over to pay for a private operation.

So, despite her deep reluctance to be indebted to her father, Flavia had succumbed to his offer, and now, three years later, she was still paying him off in the way he had demanded.

Summoned to London to play the complaisant daughter, dressed to the nines, and chit-chatting, exchanging social nothings with people she couldn't care less about but whom her father either wanted to impress or wanted to do lucrative business with. She was playing a role just as much as if she had been an actress on a stage. A role she hated for its falseness and hypocrisy, with her father treating her in public as if she were the apple of his eye, doting and devoted, when the truth was completely different.

Now, though, it was even more of an ordeal than ever. Since her hip operation, though successful, her grandmother had started to deteriorate mentally, and for the last two years her dementia had been remorselessly worsening. It meant that leaving her even for a few days, as she was doing now, made Flavia even more anxious about her. Although one of her grandmother's carers, who came in regularly to help relieve Flavia for an hour or two so that she could drive into the local market town to get the shopping and other essentials done, was staying with her, it didn't stop the anxiety nagging at her. But her father had been particularly insistent she come up to London this week.

'No bloody excuses!' he'd fumed. 'I don't give a toss about the old bat. You get yourself on the next train. I've got people coming over tomorrow evening, and it's got to look good!'

Flavia had frowned—and not just at the summons. There had been an edge to her father's voice that was new. A note of strain. Cynically, Flavia had put it down to discord between her father and his latest girlfriend, Anita, whom Flavia could see across the room, wearing a fortune around her neck. She was a demanding mistress, and maybe her avarice was beginning to grate.

The impression of her father being under new tension had

been intensified when Flavia had arrived at the apartment. He'd been shorter with her than ever, and clearly preoccupied.

But not so much that he had not gripped her elbow as the guests started to arrive.

'I've got someone particularly important turning up to-night, and I want you to keep him smiling—got it?' Her father's cold eyes had flickered over her. 'You *should* be able to hold his interest—he likes his women, and he likes them to be lookers. And that's one thing you're good for! But lose all the damn barbed wire around you—why the hell you can't be more approachable, I don't know!'

It was a familiar accusation, and one that Flavia always ignored. She was polite, she was civil, and she was sociable to her father's guests, whoever they were—but never more than that. There were limits to how much of a hypocrite she would be...

'Approachable like Anita?' Flavia had suggested sweetly, knowing how much her father hated his girlfriend's predilection for openly flirting with other men.

Annoyance had flared in his face, but he'd snapped back, 'Women like her get results! They know how to make up to a man and get what they want. *You* don't make the slightest effort. Well, tonight you'd better. Like I said, it's important.'

The edge had been back in his voice, and Flavia had wondered at it. Not that it took too much wondering. Obviously one of this evening's guests was to be someone her father intended to do some highly lucrative deal with, and when money was at stake, increasing his wealth, her father, she thought cynically, put the highest priority on it. And if that meant wanting his own daughter to smarm over some fat, ageing businessmen, it didn't bother him in the least.

Filled with distaste at her father's unsavoury tactics, Flavia had pulled away from him and gone forward to greet the first arrivals, a polite but remote smile on her face. She knew she came across as stand-offish, but there was no way she was going to ape the likes of Anita, and pout her lips and flutter her eyelashes at the influential businessmen her father wanted her to charm!

She glanced unenthusiastically over the chattering guests, and as she did so, she stilled. Something had caught her attention. Correction—some*one* had caught her attention...

He must have just arrived, for he was standing by the double doors that led out into the wide entrance hall of the huge apartment, a glass of champagne in his hand. He was looking into the crowded room, his eyes resting on someone she couldn't see from this angle. She found she was glad of it, because what she wanted to do, she realised with some dim part of her mind, was look at him.

He drew her eye, drew her focus—made it impossible for her to look away. Impossible...

Impressions stormed in her mind.

Tall—broad-shouldered—dark-haired—strong features starkly defined.

He made her want to stare, and that sent a hollowing arrow through her, stilling the breath in her throat.

There was an air about him as he stood there, one hand thrust into his trouser pocket, the other holding his champagne glass, looking tall and lean and very, *very* assured.

He was a rich man. She could see that easily. Not just because of his bespoke suit and clearly expensively cut sable hair, but because of the aura he projected, the air of supreme control.

A man to draw eyes.

Especially female eyes.

And she could see why—helplessly acknowledged the effortless power of his frame, the strongly defined features that comprised a blade of a nose, a planed jawline, a wide, mobile mouth and, above all, the dark, opaque, hooded eyes that were resting, focussed and targeted, on whoever it was he was looking at.

Who is he?

The question formed itself in her head, though the moment it did so she tried to erase it. What did it matter who he was? There were any number of people at her father's parties, and one more or less made no difference. But even as she thought it she knew it was not true. Not for this man. This man was different...

She swallowed, freeing the breath that had been stuck in her throat, and as she did she realized with a start that her pulse had quickened. Realised, too, with more than a start, with a hollowing, knifing dawning, that somehow—and she didn't know how, couldn't know how—the man's gaze had shifted, pulled away from whoever it was in the room he'd been looking at and he was now looking at *her*...

Right at her.

Instantly, instinctively, she veiled her eyes, shutting him out of her vision as if he were some kind of threatening presence—disturbing and disruptive—making herself invisible to him.

Tautly, she returned her gaze to the people she was with, and haltingly resumed her conversation. But her mind was in tumult, and when, some indeterminate time later, she heard her father's voice directed at her, she welcomed the interruption to her mental consternation.

'Flavia, my darling, over here a moment!' he called in the doting, caressing voice he always used to her in public.

Dutifully she made her way towards him, trying to put out of her head the image engraved on her retinas of the darkly disturbing man who had so riveted her. She could feel agitation increasing her heart-rate.

As she approached her father the shifting pattern of guests moved, showing that there was someone standing beside him. Her agitation spiked erratically and her eyes flared involuntarily.

It was the man who had drawn her eye—more than her eye—a moment ago. Numbly, she walked up to her father, who was smiling with a benign air. 'Darling.' Her father's hand reached for her arm and closed over it. 'I'd like to introduce you—'

Flavia let herself be pulled forward. Her mouth had gone dry again. She could hear her father saying something, but it was like a buzz in her ears. All she could focus on was the man standing with her father. The same tall, broad-shouldered, confident-stanced man she'd seen in the doorway.

'Leon Maranz. And this is my daughter, Flavia.'

Her father's voice was affectionate and indulgent, but Flavia didn't care. All she could do right now was gather her composure, which had no reason—*no reason*, she echoed vehemently—to go all to pieces like this.

With palpable effort she made herself speak, forcing herself to say what was socially required. 'How do you do, Mr Maranz?' she said. Her tone was clipped, distant. Her acknowledging glance at him was the merest flicker, the barest minimum that social courtesy demanded.

She wanted urgently to take a step back, to move away, keep her distance. Up close like this, the impression he'd made on her that she'd found so disturbing even from halfway across the room was a hundred times stronger. Just as before she took in height, easily topping six feet, and shoulders sheathed, like the rest of his lean body, with the material of a bespoke handmade suit that, like the pristine white shirt he wore, stretched across a torso that was honed and taut. He might scream 'filthy rich', but fat cat he was not...

More like a sleek-coated jaguar...

That strange, disturbing, subliminal shiver seemed to go through her again as the thought passed across the surface of her mind.

'Ms Lassiter...'

The voice acknowledging her clipped greeting was deep, almost a drawl. There was an accent to it, but not an identifiable one. She didn't need a foreign name, or a foreign accent, to know that the last thing this lean, powerful, disturbing man was British. The natural olive hue of his tanned skin, the sloe-darkness of his eyes, the sable of his hair and the strong, striking features all told her that—had told her so right from the moment she'd set eyes on him.

Her eyes flickered over him again, trying not to see him, trying to shut him out. She saw something glint briefly, swiftly gone, in his dark, black-lashed eyes—something that exacerbated the strange shiver that was still going through her.

She fought for control. *Self*-control. This was ridiculous! Absurd to be so affected by a complete stranger—some rich, foreign business acquaintance of her father that she neither knew nor cared about, nor had any reason at all to be so... so...*reactive* to!

Her spine stiffened and she could feel the motion drawing her body slightly away from Leon Maranz's powerful orbit. Withdrawing a fraction—an essential fraction. Again, just for a barest moment, she thought she saw that dark glint in his eyes come again, and vanish.

She took a breath, instinctively knowing she was being less than courteous but feeling an almost atavistic urge to get away from the impact he was having on her. She gave the barest nod of acknowledgement to his return of her greeting, then turned her head towards her father. The relief of being able to look away was palpable.

'I must check with the caterers,' she announced. 'Do excuse me.'

She could see her father's face darken, knew she was being borderline rude, but she couldn't help it. Every instinct was telling her to go—get away—right away from the man she'd just been introduced to.

Her glance flickered back to him, as brief as she could make it. His expression was empty, closed. She knew she was being impolite, but she didn't care. Couldn't afford to allow herself to care about her rudeness, her glaringly obvious reluctance to engage in any kind of social exchange with him.

'Mr Maranz.' Again the barest nod towards him, and then

she turned on her heel trying not to hurry, as she found herself wanting to do, to wave to the doors leading into the dining room, where a sumptuous buffet had been laid out by the hired caterers.

As she gained the sanctuary of the other room she felt her tension immediately ease. But not her heart-rate. That, she realised, was still elevated.

Why? Why was she reacting like this to that man?

She'd met any number of rich, foreign businessmen at her father's social gatherings—so why was this one playing havoc with her nerves?

Because none of them had ever looked the way this one did!

None of them had had those dark, saturnine looks. None of them had had that packed, powerful frame. None of them had had that air about them that spoke not just of wealth but a lot more…

But what *was* that more…?

As she made herself walk the length of the buffet, pretending to inspect it, absently lifting a silver fork here and there to occupy herself, she knew exactly what that 'more' was. Whatever name you gave it, he had it—in spades.

She took an inward breath. It didn't matter what he had, or that he had it, she told herself resolutely. And it certainly didn't matter that she'd taken one look at him and felt its impact the way she had. Leon Maranz might be the most compellingly attractive man in the universe—it was nothing to her! *Could* be nothing to her.

Her face tightened grimly. She would never, *never* have anything to do with anyone she'd met through her father! Oh, he'd been keen enough on the idea of her socialising in that way—had actively encouraged it, despite her gritty resistance to any further manipulation by him for his own ends. Leon Maranz was part of her father's world—and that meant she wanted nothing to do with him, whatever the impact he had on her!

Her expression changed. Bleakly she stared at the picture hanging on the wall above the buffet table. There was another overpowering reason why it was pointless for her to react in any way at all to Leon Maranz. Even if he'd been nothing to do with her father she *still* couldn't have anything to do with him.

She wasn't free to have anything to do with *any* man.

Sadness pierced her. Her life was not her own now—it was dedicated to her grandmother, dedicated to caring for her in this the twilight of her life. It was her grandmother who needed her, and after all her grandmother had done in raising her, caring for her and loving her, devoting her life to her, she would never, never abandon her!

Flavia's eyes shadowed. Day by day the dementia was increasing, taking away more and more of the grandmother she loved so much, and whilst it broke her heart to see her declining, it was even worse to think of what must inevitably one day happen. But until that time came she would look after her grandmother—whatever it took. Including, she knew, dancing to her father's tune like this.

Other than these brief, unwelcome periods away from home, she would confine her life entirely to the needs of her grandmother, stay constantly at her side. She would do nothing that wasn't in her grandmother's best interests. And if that meant denying herself the kind of life that she might have been leading as an independent solo woman of twenty-five—well, she would accept that.

So it really didn't matter a jot that her father's guest had had such a powerful impact on her—it was completely irrelevant! Leon Maranz was nothing to do with her, *could* be nothing to her, and would stay that way.

She gave a little shake of her head. For heaven's sake—just because he'd had an impact on her, obviously it didn't mean she'd had an impact on *him*. OK, so he'd seen her looking at him when he'd been standing near the doorway, but so what? With looks like his, a magnetically brooding presence like

his, every other women here would have done the same—
were doubtless doing it right now! All she had to do was get
a grip, stop reacting to him in this ridiculous way, and avoid
him for the rest of the evening. Simple.

'Tell me, are you always so short with your guests?'

She spun round, dismay and shock etched in her face.

Leon Maranz was standing not a metre away from her
in the empty room. His expression, she could see instantly,
was forbidding. Equally instantly every resolution she'd just
made about getting a grip on her composure and not reacting
to him utterly vanished. She could feel herself go into urgent
self-protective, defensive mode. She stiffened.

'I beg your pardon?'

The words might be polite, might theoretically mean what
they were saying, but her tone implied utterly the opposite. It
was as freezing and as clipped as if she was cutting the words
out of the air with a pair of the sharpest scissors.

His expression hardened at the icy tone. 'You should,' he
said. 'What reason did you have for snubbing me when your
father introduced me?'

'I didn't snub you!' She spoke shortly, aware with part
of her mind that she was once again bordering on rudeness,
even though she didn't mean to be. But her nerves were on
edge—yet again. His presence seemed to generate such an
overpowering reaction in her she couldn't cope well with it.

He raised a sardonic eyebrow. 'What do you do when you
do snub someone, then?' There was a taunt in his voice, but
beneath the taunt was another note. Something she could rec-
ognise because she knew there was justification for it.

Anger.

For a moment, just the briefest moment, she almost made
a decision to do what she knew she must—apologise. Mol-
lify him with a soft word. Defuse the situation. But even as
she made that resolve, she made the fatal mistake of meeting his eyes.

And in them was an expression that she'd have recognised even if she'd been blind.

She'd have felt it on her skin—felt it in the sudden heat of her blood, the quickening of her pulse. Felt the wash of his eyes, the open message in them. Felt the breathless congestion in her chest.

He was looking her over...signalling his sexual interest in her...making it plain...

For one long, disastrous moment she was helpless, out of control, taking the full force of what was being directed at her. She could feel the hot, tumid breathlessness in her lungs, the flare of heat in her veins, and then—even worse—the betraying flush of her skin. A tautening all through her body, as if a flame were licking over her...

She couldn't move. Couldn't break away from the eyes holding hers.

Then slowly, deliberately, he smiled. Lines indented around his mouth, emphasising the strong blade of his nose, the sensual twist of his lips. Long lashes swept briefly down over his sloe-dark eyes.

'Shall we start again, Ms Lassiter?' he murmured, and the deep, faintly accented voice was rich with satisfaction.

And she knew why—because he now knew *exactly* the reason she'd been so short with him. Had found a reason for it that brought that sensual smile to his lips. The smile that was playing havoc with her resolve to be immune to him, to have nothing whatsoever to do with him!

For one endless moment her mind hung in the balance. All she had to do was smile back. Let the stiffness of her spine soften...let the rejection in her eyes dissolve. Accept her reaction to him...accept what he was so clearly offering her. The opportunity to share what was flaring between them so powerfully, so enticingly, to explore with him a new, sensual world that she had never before encountered but which was now drawing her like an enticing flame...

No!

It was impossible! Unthinkable. Leon Maranz moved in a world she didn't want to have anything to do with. The slick, shallow, glossy, money-obsessed world her father inhabited, which was nothing to do with the reality of *her* life—a reality that had no room in it for any priority other than her grandmother. A life that could have no place for Leon Maranz or anything he offered.

No place!

Which meant it was time to stop this now. Right now.

Before it's too late...

The disturbing words whispered in her head, and she knew she had to cut them out—decisively and sharply. Stop what must not start.

'I don't think so, Mr Maranz.'

Her voice was like a scalpel, severing the air between them. Severing the opportunity to negate the rudeness she knew he did not deserve, but which she was driven to deliver from a sense of urgent, primitive self-preservation.

Because if she didn't—if she allowed him to get through to her, to smile at her...smile *with* her...get past her defences—then what would happen?

What would happen if she let him 'start again'?

The question rang inside her head, demanding an answer. An answer she refused to give. Not now—not when the adrenaline was pumping in her veins and dominating her mind, urging her to do the only sensible, safe thing even if it meant being rude. She needed to minimise her exposure to this man by any means possible.

She gave a small smile, tight and insincere—dismissive. 'Do please excuse me...'

She walked off, unbearable tension in her back, knowing with a cold burning in her body that she had behaved inexcusably rudely, but knowing she had had to do so. Because the alternative—the one that she'd thrust out of her head urgently, ruthlessly—was unthinkable.

Quite, quite unthinkable.

Behind her, as he watched her threading her way back into the crowded, opulent reception room, Leon Maranz stood, his face tight.

Anger was spiking in him. Yet again she'd blanked him! Cut him dead. Then walked off as if he didn't exist!

His eyes, watching her stalk back into the main reception room, darkened to black slits. Emotion seethed in him as she disappeared from view. Her rudeness was breathtaking! Unbelievable!

Who the hell does she think she is to do that to me? To hand that out to me? Talk to me in that way?

Once again he felt that old, suffocating, burning sensation in his chest that he'd used to feel long years ago. He had thought it would never strike him again. Yet at Flavia Lassiter's curt dismissiveness it had reared up in familiar, ugly fashion. Bringing with it memories he didn't want. Memories he'd left far, far behind.

He fought it back, mastering the destructive, dark emotion, refusing to let it poison his mind. It was unnecessary to evoke it now—that burning sense of being looked down on, looked through, that had evoked his burst of anger at her. No, her rude rebuff of him was not for *that* reason. He forced control over his wayward reaction to her cutting rejection, subduing it. In its place he reached for an alternative—an explanation for her rudeness, her dismissal of him, that was far more palatable to him. One he could seize on.

Every masculine instinct told him there *was* another, quite different reason for her behaviour. One he should welcome, not resent. Her glacial attitude might have attempted to freeze him out, but all it had done was reinforce a quite different interpretation.

It was only a mask. A mask she had adopted in an attempt—however futile!—to conceal from him her true reaction to him. A reaction he had seen flare betrayingly in her eyes as he had smiled at her. It had told him exactly what he'd wanted to know, confirmed what he had felt with every masculine instinct, with all his years of experience in feminine response—a reaction that mirrored his to her.

Desire.

A simple, brief word, but it was the one he wanted—the only one he wanted. Nothing else. Because desire was the only emotion he wanted to associate with Flavia Lassiter. Everything else about her could be put aside as unnecessary for what he wanted. And pointless—and destructive.

The anger that had spiked in him as she'd stalked away ebbed away completely, the bunched tension in his muscles relaxing. There was no need for either anger or tension. No need at all. He was sure of it. Flavia Lassiter could be as dismissive of him as she liked, but it was only a mask—a futile attempt to deny what it was useless for her to deny. The fact that everything about her told him she was as responsive to him as he was to her.

Tension eased from his shoulders. His features lightened. He strolled back into the main reception room, a strategy forming rapidly in his mind. For now he would let her be. It was clear to him she was fighting his impact on her, and that she was resisting facing up to it. OK, it *was* sudden. He allowed that. And for a woman like her, clearly used to being in strict control of herself, adept at presenting an outwardly composed and indifferent front, that was understandable. For the moment, then, she could stay safely behind the crystalline shield she was holding him at bay with. When the time was right he would shatter it completely. And get from her exactly what he knew with complete certainty now he definitely wanted...

As did she...

It was just a matter of time before she accepted it. That was all. A slight smile started to play around Leon's mouth. The prospect of persuading her was very, very enjoyable.

CHAPTER TWO

How Flavia got through the rest of the evening she didn't know. It seemed to go on for ever. She kept a perpetual eye open for Leon Maranz, and was grateful he seemed to be keeping himself away from her. She could see her father with him and Anita sometimes—clearly more than happy to be so—but more often than that he was surrounded by any number of other guests. Especially female ones, she noticed without surprise and with a distinct tightening of her mouth. She avoided her father as well, because the last thing she wanted was to have him grill her on why she'd been so short to his favoured guest.

Her avoidance continued even when the endless party finally wound down, the guests all left, and her father and Anita headed off to a nightclub. Whether or not Leon Maranz had gone with them she didn't know, and refused to care. She could feel only relief that he had gone, and that the ordeal of the evening was finally over.

The moment she could, Flavia disappeared into her bedroom. For the first time since her gaze had lighted on Leon Maranz that evening she started to feel the tension ebb out of her. Safe at last, she thought with relief.

But as she stood under the shower some minutes later she had cause to question that assumption. Leon Maranz might be out of the apartment but he was not out of her head. Far from it…

The water pouring over her naked body was not helping—running down her torso, between the valley of her breasts, down her flanks, her limbs... It was a sensuous experience that she was all too aware was the last thing she should be experiencing when trying to put out of her head the image of the man who had caught her attention, impacted upon her as no other man had.

As she massaged shower gel into her skin, its warm soapy suds laving her body, she could feel her breasts reacting, see in her mind's eye those dark hooded eyes resting on her as if he were viewing her naked body...

No!

It was insane to let her mind conjure such things! Leon Maranz wasn't going to see her again, let alone see her naked body, for heaven's sake! Time to put him totally out of her mind.

With a sharp movement she switched the shower dial to cool and doused herself in chilly water, then snapped the flow off completely. Stepping out of the stall, she grabbed a bath-towel and rubbed herself dry with brisk, no-nonsense vigour. It was completely irrelevant that Leon Maranz had had the effect on her that he had! It was an effect every woman there had shared, so she was hardly unique. And even if—*if*, she instructed herself ruthlessly—he had made it clear in that brief, fraught exchange by the buffet that he was eyeing her up, that only made it *more* imperative that she put him completely out of her head!

Nothing can come of this and nothing is going to. That is that. End of.

She dropped her towel, donned her nightdress, and climbed into bed. Then she reached for her mobile. Time to check with Mrs Stephens on how her grandmother had been this evening.

Familiar anxiety stabbed in her mind, displacing her troubling thoughts about Leon Maranz and his disturbing impact on her with even more troubled thoughts. The constant worry she felt about her grandmother surfaced again through the layers of her ridiculous obsessing about a man who meant absolutely nothing to her, whom she'd only seen for a few hours, and exchanged only a few words with.

Angry with herself for the way she'd reacted that evening, when there were real worries and concerns for her to focus on about the one person she loved in this world, she settled herself into bed and phoned home. It was late, she knew, but Mrs Stephens would be awake, and these days her grandmother could be awake for hours into the night sometimes. It was one of the things that made it so wearing to care for her, Flavia admitted, labour of love though it was for her.

When she spoke to the carer Flavia was relieved to hear that her grandmother was quite soporific, and seemed not to have realised her granddaughter was not in the house. It was a blessing, Flavia knew, because it would have made these visits to London at her father's behest even less endurable knowing that her grandmother was at home, fretting for her.

What did cause her grandmother unbearable distress, though, was being away from home herself. Flavia had discovered that when, some six months ago, her grandmother had had a fall and had had to spend a week in hospital being checked over and monitored. It had been dreadful to see how agitated and disturbed her grandmother had become, trying to get out of the hospital bed, her mental state anguished, tearful. Several times she'd been found wandering around the ward incoherent, visibly searching for something, distressed and flailing around.

Yet the moment she'd come back home to Harford the agitation had left her completely and she'd reverted to the much calmer, happier, and more contented person that her form of dementia allowed her to be. From then on Flavia had known that above all her grandmother had to remain in the familiar, reassuring surroundings where she had lived for over fifty years, since coming to Harford as a young bride. Whatever the dimness in her mind, she seemed to know that she was at home, and presumably it felt safe and familiar to her there, wandering happily around, or just sitting quietly, gazing out over the gardens she had once loved to tend.

Flavia gave a sad smile. It still pained her to see her beloved grandmother so mentally and physically frail, but she knew that at the end of a long life her grandmother was starting to take her leave of it. Just when that would happen no one could say, except that it was coming ever closer. Flavia was determined that, come what may, if it was at all medically possible her grandmother would die in her own home, with her granddaughter at her side.

Her gaze grew distant as she stared blankly at the far wall opposite the bed. Just what she would do once her grandmother died was still uncertain, but she knew she would do her very best to hang on to Harford. She loved it far too much to let it go. Her plan was to run it as an upmarket holiday let, though it would require modernising for the bathrooms and kitchen, plus general refurbishment—all of which would require some kind of upfront financing, on top of coping with the inevitable death duties. One thing was certain, though— her father wouldn't offer her a penny to help.

Not that she would take it. It was bad enough owing him for her grandmother's hip operation, let alone anything else. Her father, she thought bitterly, was *not* a good man to be in hock to... Who knew how he might wield such power over her head?

She reached out to turn off the bedside light. There was no point thinking about anything other than her current concerns. Her grandmother's needs were her priority, and that was that. There was no room in her life for anything else.

Any*one* else....

Yet as she slowly sank into slumber echoes seemed to be hazing in her memory—a deep, drawling voice, a strong-featured face, dark, unreadable eyes...holding hers...

Leon Maranz poured himself a brandy, swirling it absently in his hand. His face was shuttered.

He was alone in his apartment, though he might easily have had companionship. He knew enough women in London who would have rushed to his side at the merest hint of a request for their company. Even at Lassiter's cocktail party he could have had his pick had he wanted to. Including—he gave an acid smile devoid of humour—Lassiter's current *inamorata*, who had shown her interest and looked openly disappointed when he'd declined her pressing suggestion that he accompany them to a nightclub.

What would she have done, he thought cynically, had he decided to amuse himself by inviting her back here? Would she have played the affronted female and gone rushing back to her ageing lover's side? Or would the temptation to gain a lover much, much richer than Lassiter—and so much closer to her in age have overcome whatever scruples she had left in life? And what would Lassiter himself have done? Tolerated the man he so badly wanted to do business with bedding his own mistress? His cynicism deepened.

Not that he would have put either of the pair to such a test. Anita's bleached-blonde, over-made-up looks had no allure for him—nor the voluptuous figure so blatantly on display. When it came to women his tastes were far more selective compared to the likes of Lassiter.

An image flickered in his mind's eye as he slowly swirled the brandy in its glass. Flavia Lassiter was cut from a quite different cloth than her father's overdone mistress.

Contemplatively Leon let his mind delineate her figure, her fine-boned features that were of such exceptional quality. The very fact that she did not flaunt her beauty had only served to draw his eye to her the more. Did she not realise that? Did she not see that hers was a rare beauty that could not be concealed, could not be repressed or denied? Leon's dark eyes glinted as he raised his brandy glass to his nose, savouring the heady bouquet. She could not repress or deny what she had betrayed when she'd met his gaze, what had been evident to him—blazingly so—in the flare of her pupils, the slight but revealing parting of her lips. She had responded to him just as he to her. That had told him everything he needed to know...

His expression hardened. The curt disdain she had handed out, dismissing him, burned like a brand in his mind. Had it indeed been nothing more than an attempt to deny her response to his interest in her—for reasons he could not fathom? Since he did not intend that denial to persist he could afford to ignore it. An expression entered his eyes that had not been there for many, many years. Or had it been the result of something quite different? Something he had not encountered for a long time, but which could still slide like a knife through the synapses of his memory.

Like clips from an old movie, memories shaded through his mind, taking him far, far away from where he was now. To a world...a universe away from where he was standing in this five-star hotel suite, wearing a hand-tailored suit costing thousands, enjoying the finest vintage brandy and everything else that his wealth could give him effortlessly, in as much abundance as he wanted.

His life had not always been like that...

It was the cold he could remember. The bitter, biting cold of Europe in winter. Icy wind cutting through the thin material of his shabby clothes. The crowded, anonymous streets of the city where he was just one more homeless, desperate denizen, pushed aside, ignored, resented.

Making his way slowly and painfully in that harsh, bleak world, grabbing what jobs he could, however menial, however hard, however badly paid—jobs that the citizens of the country he had come to did not want to do, that were beneath them, but not beneath the desperate immigrants and refugees grateful to get them.

He had become used to being looked down on, looked through as if he did not exist, as if those looking through him didn't *want* him to exist. He had got used to it—but he had never, even in his poorest days, swallowed it easily. It had made him angry, had driven him ever onwards, helping to fire and fuel his determination to make something of himself, to ensure that one day no one would look through him, no one would think him invisible.

Yet even now, it seemed, his hand tightening unconsciously around the brandy glass, when he moved in a stratospheric world with ease and assurance, that anger, the cause of which was long, long gone, still possessed some power over him...

Why? That was the question that circled in his mind now, as he stood in his luxurious hotel suite, savouring the vintage brandy, enjoying the bountiful fruits of his hard work, his determination and drive. Why should that anger still come? Why should it have a power over him?

And who was *she* to have the ability to revive that anger? Who was she, that upper-crust daughter of Alistair Lassiter, to look through him as if he were as invisible as the impoverished immigrant he had once been? Someone to serve drinks, clear tables, to wait hand and foot on wealthy women like her? Who was she to blank him, snub him, consign him to the ranks of those whose existence was barely acknowledged?

He could feel his anger stab like the fiery heat of the brandy in his throat. Then, forcing himself to lessen his grip on the glass, he inhaled deeply, taking back control of his emotions, subduing that bite of anger. The anger was unnecessary. Because surely, he argued, his first explanation of Flavia Lassiter's coldness was the correct one—she was fighting her own response to him, and it was *that* that had made her avoid meeting his eyes, made her so curt towards him. That was the explanation he must adhere to. For reasons he as yet found unfathomable, but would not for very much longer, she was trying to hold him at bay.

A cynical glint gleamed in his eye. Alistair Lassiter would be overjoyed by his interest in his daughter. He would see it, Leon thought cynically, as an opportune way of keeping him close—something Lassiter was extremely keen to do.

The cynical glint deepened. Right now Maranz Finance was Lassiter's best hope of saving his sinking, profligate business empire from complete collapse...

CHAPTER THREE

FLAVIA was sitting, tight-lipped, in the back of her father's limo. Her face was set. On the other side of her father, Anita leant forward.

'You look *so* good, sweetie, with your hair down and some red lippy,' she informed Flavia, sounding pleased with herself. 'It really jazzes up that dress.' As her false eyelashes swept up and down over Flavia, they cast a critical eye over the gown the younger woman was wearing. 'Great style— just a shame about the draggy colour.'

Flavia's expression changed minutely. She'd been despatched with Anita that afternoon by her father to buy herself 'something glamorous for a change' as he'd snapped at her, looking the worse for wear after his late night, his eyes bloodshot and his face puffy.

Flavia had objected, but her father had been adamant.

'We're going to a flash charity bash tonight, and just for a damn change I don't want you dressing like a nun!'

Knowing Anita's predilection for bling, Flavia had been on her guard, and when the other woman had picked out a clingy scarlet number she'd at least succeeded in swapping it for a pale aqua version at the counter, while Anita had been trying on the ruched and sequinned purple gown she was poured into now. Discovering the colour swap when Flavia had emerged from a bedroom before setting off had so annoyed Anita, however, that she'd managed to unpin Flavia's tightly knotted chignon and flash her own bright red lipstick over her mouth just as Alistair Lassiter was hurrying them out of the apartment to the waiting limo.

He was visibly on edge, Flavia could tell—but then she was as well. The moment they arrived at the Park Lane hotel where the charity event was being held she would dive into the Ladies' and wipe Anita's vivid lipstick off her, and repin her hair.

But her intentions were foiled. As they made their way into the hotel Anita's hand fastened around her wrist. 'Don't even *think* about it!' she breathed, and her hand remained clamped where it was.

Stiffly, feeling self-conscious enough as it was in the bias-cut gown, let alone with her hair loose and heaven only knew how much garish lipstick, Flavia had no option but to let herself be swept forward into the banqueting hall. They were, as her father had complained, running late, and everyone except a few other latecomers like themselves had already taken their seats at the appointed tables.

Threading her way towards their table, flanked by her father and Anita, Flavia could only determine a sea of people and hear a wave of chatter and the clink of glasses and rustle of gowns. Her father was greeting people here and there, and Anita was waving conspicuously at people she knew, too, while Flavia looked neither to left or right. When they reached their table, with their three places waiting for them, she slipped into the seat on her father's right hand side with a sense of relief.

The relief lasted less than a second.

'Ms Lassiter…'

The deep, accented voice on her right made her head whip round.

Leon Maranz was seated beside her.

Emotion sliced through her. Shock and dismay were uppermost. But beneath both another emotion stabbed. Instantly she fought to subdue it, but the physical impact was too great, and she could feel that treacherous quickening of her blood. Feel, even more powerfully, the urge to get to her feet and bolt.

Why—why was she reacting like this to the man? It was absurd to be so...so...

So...what, exactly? She flailed around in her mind, trying to find the word she needed. Trying to blank out the way she was reacting. Trying to wipe the dismay and shock from her face. Trying to gather her composure and force herself to do what she had to do—which was simply to nod civilly, politely, courteously and nothing more than that. Nothing at all.

'Mr...Maranz, isn't it?' She hesitated over his name, as if she had difficulty recalling it. Then she made a show of flicking open her linen napkin and spreading it over her knees. She was grateful, for once, for her father's presence, as he leant across her.

'Ah—Leon. Good to see you!' he said effusively. 'I'm so pleased you accepted my invitation to be my guest here tonight.'

At Flavia's side Leon Maranz's eyes glittered darkly, and he found himself reconsidering his decision to attend the function as Lassiter's guest. Despite his attraction to Flavia Lassiter, *should* he have come this evening? Yes, she had made an immediate impact on him the moment he'd set eyes on her, but was it truly a good idea to pursue his interest in her? The glitter in his eyes intensified. Especially since it meant he would have to spend time in Alistair Lassiter's overattentive company this evening.

Even if he did decide to invest in his business, socialising with the man was not necessary—unless, of course, it was a means to an end in respect of his daughter...

On that note, it was clear from her frosty reception of his greeting that she was still very much on her guard with him. Was it truly worth his time and effort to thaw that freezing demeanour? Yet even as he considered it he knew, with a little stab of emotion, that seeing her again had in no way lessened his response to her. Indeed, it had been accentuated...

He had had time only for a moment's appreciation, but that had been enough to confirm that the sinuous gown she was wearing, baring shoulders over which the shimmering fall of her loosened hair was cascading, not to mention the sensuous, vivid scarlet of her mouth, were a stunning enhancement of the beauty he'd seen last night. Tonight, he thought appreciatively, there was no question of her seeking to subdue her beauty with the severity of her dress or sedate maquillage. The effect was—stunning.

Decision raced through him. Yes, Flavia Lassiter, despite her father, was well worth pursuing.

As for her father—well, he would put up with him as best he could this evening, and for the moment reserve judgement on whether he would supply the bail-out that Lassiter was so desperately in need of.

Leon's mouth pressed to a thin line. What kind of fool was Alistair Lassiter to have got himself into such an irretrievable mess? The global recession should have made him cautious, but instead Lassiter had taken unwarrantable risks—too many of them—and his spending had been lavish. Now he was teetering on the brink of complete collapse. Now he was going to have to rely on a turnaround specialist like Maranz Finance to rescue him.

Leon's eyes were veiled. *Would* he bail out Lassiter? How much real value was there left in the company? And was it worth the trouble to secure it? Lassiter was walking on thin ice. Far too many of his assets, as Leon knew perfectly well from his own investigations, were paper-thin and his debt was punitive. For all the surface gloss he still reflected, Alistair Lassiter had precious little beneath. Even the Regent's Park apartment was mortgaged up to the hilt, and his other personal properties had already been sold off.

While he decided whether to bail out Lassiter he would further his interest in his daughter. He levelled his veiled gaze on her as she reached for a bottle of sparkling water and poured some into her glass. Waiters were already circling with white wine, but she'd covered her glass with her palm, giving her head a slight shake. Did she eschew all alcohol? Leon wondered.

'You don't drink wine?' he enquired.

She seemed to start at his words, and her head jerked around.

'Very seldom,' she answered, her voice clipped. She made to turn her head away again, as if that were all she were going to say on the subject.

'Empty calories?' Leon's voice was bland.

'Yes.'

She lifted her glass of water, aware of how stiffly she had spoken. But then her spine was as stiff as a poker right now. Why on earth had her father not told her he'd invited Leon Maranz this evening? The answer was obvious, of course. He hadn't wanted her to know because he hadn't wanted her to be warned beforehand. And now here she was, trapped between them, wearing a dress she didn't want to be wearing, with her hair hanging down her back and her mouth covered in vivid lipstick.

She raised her napkin and made a show of dabbing her lips after drinking, covertly attempting to dab off some of the sticky red layer. Beside her she was aware—ultra-aware—of Leon Maranz's eyes on her.

How on earth am I going to get through the evening?

The question was uppermost in her mind. Closely followed by its companion.

Why am I being like this?

She had met plenty of men her father wanted her to take an interest in for his sake, but she had never freaked out like this before! She had always managed to be indifferent, without being so ridiculously tongue-tied and affected. So why was she being like this with this man?

But then, she acknowledged, with a hollow sensation inside her, no one her father had tried to set her up with before had been anything like Leon Maranz.

No one could be...

The words formed in her mind, shaping themselves. No one could possibly have the kind of impact he had. It hadn't lessened in the slightest in the twenty-four hours since she had first experienced it. Instead it had intensified. She could feel it like a kind of forcefield. She was far, far too close to him for a start—hyper-aware of him only a few inches away from her at the table, knowing she only had to tilt her head slightly to see him, instead of straining forward, apparently finding the floral arrangement in the middle of the table absolutely fascinating.

But she could still sense him there sitting beside her, his powerful frame set off by the tuxedo, see from the corner of her eye his large, tanned hand reaching for his wine. Nor was sight the only sense he impinged upon. The deep, accented drawl of his voice was resonating in her head as well. And there was another sense, too, more subtle, yet there all the same. His raw, male scent assaulted her, overlaid by the slightest hint of something citrus, musky, in his aftershave.

She tried to blank it out but it was impossible. Just as blanking out his presence beside her was impossible, however doggedly she stared ahead and toyed with her water. The only mercy was that, thankfully, he seemed to have accepted her reluctance to engage in any conversation with him, however trivial, and had turned his attention to the woman on the other side of him. Flavia could hear her light tinkle of laughter, though what they were talking about she neither knew nor cared.

'Leon! I must have your opinion!'

Anita's piercing voice cut across her, demanding his attention. Flavia could have slapped her for it.

He turned towards her again, away from the woman on his right.

'On what?' he replied. His voice seemed reserved.

Anita flapped a heavily beringed hand. 'Don't you think

Flavia looks so much better with her hair loose rather than pinned up the way it was last night?'

Like two burning brands Flavia felt her cheeks flare. Anger and mortification warred within her. She wanted to snap viciously at Anita, but Leon Maranz was replying.

'Very…uninhibited,' he drawled, and Flavia could feel, like a physical touch, his eyes working over her.

The brands in her cheeks burnt fiercer.

'You see?' Anita's voice was triumphant. 'I told you, Flavia. You could look a knock-out if you tried more! I tell you, darling,' she said, 'if you can persuade Leon Maranz to admire you, you've got it made!' She gave a gush of laughter as insincere as it was overdone.

Flavia's expression iced over.

It remained like ice for the whole of the eternally long meal—it was the only way she could get through it.

She was given some mercy—Anita laid off her, and Leon Maranz, when he wasn't talking to the woman on his right, or to the other guests across the table who seemed keen to engage his attention, talked to her father. Or rather, she realised, her father talked to Leon Maranz. The edginess he'd displayed earlier seemed to have vanished, and now he was in effusive mode, she could tell, mingling loud bonhomie with an eager attentiveness that told Flavia that, whatever potential use Leon Maranz was to him, it was considerable.

Was it reciprocated? she wondered as she steadily ate through the courses, despite a complete lack of appetite. Eating was easier than talking. So was being aware of what her father was doing.

But on what Leon Maranz was doing she was far less clear. There was no evidence of reciprocation, no evidence of anything except the fact that Leon Maranz seemed to prefer her father to do the talking. His laconic answers only seemed to drive her father onward. He was getting more and more exuberant—or, a sudden thought struck her, should that be more and more desperate?

She glanced sideways at her father. He'd loosened his bow tie slightly and his cheeks were reddening, his eyes becoming pouchy. His glass was frequently refilled, and Flavia wondered how much he'd had to drink. Distaste flickered in her face. Thank God she was going back home tomorrow. She couldn't wait to get away from her father, away from the shallow, money-obsessed life he lived. However worthy the cause of this evening's function, she didn't want to be here in this vast ornate banqueting room, with the scent of wine and flowers and expensive perfume everywhere, the glint of jewellery on the women and the sleek, fat-cat look of the men.

She wanted to be at home, at Harford, deep in her beloved countryside. Back with her grandmother in the quiet, familiar world so very dear to her…so very precious…

But for now all she could do was tough it out—get through the evening however long it seemed.

After an interminable length of time the meal and the fund-raising presentations from the charity directors finally drew to a close, with coffeepots and *petits-fours* and an array of liqueurs being placed on the tables. At the far end of the huge room on a little stage a band had formed, and was starting to strike up.

Flavia closed her eyes, trying to shut it all out. She wanted out of here. Now. But it wasn't going to happen. She knew that. And she also knew, with a heaviness that was tangible, that Anita and her father were going to head off to the dance floor, and she would be left with Leon Maranz. Unless—dear God, *please*, she found herself praying—he went off with someone else. But the woman on his other side had got up to dance as well, with her partner, and with a hollowing sensation Flavia realised that she was now sitting next to Leon Maranz with empty seats on either side of them.

Stiffly she reached for the coffeepot.

'Allow me.'

His hand was before her, lifting the heavy pot as though it weighed nothing and pouring coffee into her empty cup.

'Cream?' The drawling voice was solicitous.

She gave a minute shake of her head.

'Of course—more empty calories,' he murmured.

She shot him a look. It was a mistake.

A mistake, a mistake, a *mistake*.

He lounged back in his chair, one hand cupping a brandy glass. There was an air of relaxation about him, and yet there was something else that told Flavia at some alien, atavistic, visceral level of her being that he was not relaxed at all. That he was merely giving the impression of being relaxed.

It was in his eyes. They were heavy-lidded, yet she could see that they were resting on her with an expression that was not in the least somnolent.

For a second, almost overpoweringly, she wanted to get to her feet and run—run far and fast, right out of the building. But she couldn't. It was impossible. She couldn't do something so obviously, outrageously socially unacceptable.

She could head for the Ladies' Room, though.

She seized on the notion with relief. That would be OK— in fact it would be ideal, because then she could pin her hair up and make sure any trace of Anita's lipstick was gone.

She steeled herself to stand up, but before her stiffened limbs could move Leon Maranz pushed back his chair and surveyed her. His eyes moved back to hers, holding them effortlessly, and in the space of time it took to lock eyes with him she became paralysed, unable to move, breathe, to do anything at all except read in his dark obsidian eyes the unmistakable glint of an unmissable message.

Desire.

It was as flagrant as his audacity in letting his long-lashed eyes rest on her like a physical caress.

Tangible. Intimate…

She thrust up from her chair, stood up, every muscle taut like a wire under impossible tension. She had to go—right now.

'Do please excuse me. I really must…'

Her voice was high and clipped and breathless. Thoughts seared through her mind.

I can't cope with this! It's too flagrant, too overpowering, and it's all far, far too impossible! Impossible to have anything to do with a man from my father's world! Impossible to have anything to do with any man when my overwhelming responsibility is for my grandmother. So it doesn't matter—doesn't matter a jot what this ridiculous reaction to him is, I can't let it go anywhere, and I have to stop it in its tracks now. Right now!

But he wasn't to be evaded. Instead he matched her gesture, getting to his feet in a lithe, effortless movement, towering over her. Too close—much too close. She stepped back, trying not to bump into the empty chair beside her.

'You know…' he said, and his voice was a deep, dark drawl that set her nerve-endings vibrating at some weird, subliminal frequency. His eyes did not relinquish hers, did not allow her to tear her gaze away from his. 'I don't think I *do* excuse you, Ms Lassiter. Not two nights in a row.' The dark glint in his eye was shot through with something that upped that strange subliminal frequency. 'This time I think I will just do—*this*.'

He moved so fast she did not see it coming. His hand fastened around her wrist. Not tightly, not gripping it, but encircling it…imprisoning it.

He looked down at her, even taller somehow, his shoulders broader, his eyes darker.

'I'd like to dance with you,' he said.

He drew her hand into the crook of his arm so that her hand splayed involuntarily on the dark sleeve of his tuxedo jacket, her nails white against the smooth black cloth. She wanted to jerk free, tear herself away, but he was looking down at her still, a taunting smile playing on his lips.

'You don't want to make a scene, do you, Ms Lassiter?' he said, and a saturnine eyebrow quirked. The dark eyes were glinting. Mocking.

Emotion flashed in her eyes. For a wild and impossible moment, she wanted to do exactly what he'd said she could not—tug her hand free of its imprisonment, push away from him, storm off in a swirl of skirts and leave him standing there.

But there were too many people around. This was a formal function, with people who knew him, knew her father, knew who *she* was. Too many eyes were coming their way. Heads were turning at other tables set too close by.

He saw her dilemma, mocked it, and started to draw her away, towards the dance floor beyond. He could feel the stiffness of her body, the anger in the set of her shoulders. Well, he had anger of his own. Anger because she had spent the entire meal as if he did not exist, blanking him out, doing her best to ignore him, refusing to see him, talk to him. Refusing to do anything except the one thing she could not refuse.

She could not refuse to react to him.

Satisfaction—shot with grimness—spiked through him. That was the one thing she could not do. She could not hide her body's response to him. A response that shimmered from her just from his presence at her side, despite the tense straining of her body away from his.

They reached the dance floor. She resisted him every step of the way, but was helpless to do anything about it lest she break that unspoken code of her class—never make a scene, never draw attention to yourself, never break the rules of social engagement. And he would use that code ruthlessly for his own advantage—to get what he wanted. To draw her to him.

'Shall we?'

The taunt was in his low voice even as he turned her towards him, slipping a hand around her waist. His other hand clasped hers and he started to move her into the dance.

Helpless, Flavia could do nothing—nothing at all—to stop him.

Inside her breast, emotions stormed.

It was like being in torment—a torment that was lacerating every nerve-ending in her body. Everything about her body seemed to be registering physical sensation at double—triple—the intensity. She could feel his hand at her waist as if it were a brand, her hand clasped in his as if it were encased in steel. Steel sheathed in smoothest velvet.

And he was too close to her! Far, far too close! He was holding her, guiding her, turning her into the movements of the dance so that his body was counterpoised to hers, and hers was encircling his. Around and around they moved to the lush rhythm of the music, weaving through the press of other dancers. He was bending her pliantly into the dance, though her body felt as stiff as wood, and she could feel every muscle in her body seeking to strain away from him. It was as if he was endlessly drawing her towards him and she was endlessly resisting him, yet pinioned at her waist by the heat and pressure of his hand against her spine, the velvet steel of his hand around hers.

He was holding her captive.

And there was nothing she could do about it! Unless she broke free by force, tore herself away from him and stormed from the dance floor. And she couldn't do that. Couldn't because it would make a fuss, make a scene, draw eyes to her...

Couldn't because she didn't want to...

For a second—one fatal moment as the knowledge knifed through her brain like the edge of a sword, cleaving through her consciousness—she felt the tension in her body dissolve. Felt her body become pliant, supple.

And he felt it, too. She knew that he felt it, too, by the sudden flaring of his eyes to which she had suddenly lifted hers instead of what she was supposed to be doing, which was to stare rigidly, stonily over his shoulder.

Shock was in her gaze, and then that too dissolved, and she could feel the weight of her body shift as his hand at her waist seemed to deepen its support of her suddenly relaxed body. His fingers splayed out and she could feel each one fanning across her back, the thin silky material of her dress no barrier at all. And now his dark eyes held hers as she gazed

helplessly across at him, feeling the warmth of his hand at
her back, the warmth of his clasp on her other hand.

'You see...?'

His voice was low and intimate—disturbingly intimate,
below the level of the music and the conversation all around
them. There was a smile—knowing, satisfied—playing at
his mouth as he spoke to her. He knew what she was doing,
what she was feeling, how her body was reacting to his, how
the rest of the world was disappearing, how there was nothing left except themselves, turning slowly together in each
other's arms.

Each other's embrace.

Like a string jerking tight she strained away again, tensing
all the lines of her body, maximising the distance between
them, stiff and rigid once more. Her eyes cut away, gazed un-
seeingly out over the room; her lips compressed, hardening
the contours of her face.

The music stopped, and she felt the tension racking her
body lessen. Relief filled her that her torment was over. Impulsively she tugged her hand free, stepping away from him,
not caring if the gesture was too abrupt for social usage. She
couldn't afford to care.

'Do please excuse me.' Her voice was clipped and she
would not look at him. Would not do anything except escape
from the dance floor.

She threaded her way as rapidly as she could towards the
doors that led out to the foyer, where she knew the powder
room was. The ballroom was a blur, her only focus on gain-
ing the haven of the Ladies'. Inside, she collapsed down on
a velvet-covered stool in the vanity section of the spacious
facilities.

Her reflection dismayed her.

Even in demure aqua, the bias cut of the dress did its
work—far too well! It sheathed her body with glistening wa-
tered silk, its narrow straps showing too much bare shoulder

and arm and—for her—too much décolletage, modest though it was by Anita's sultry standards.

But Anita's damage was worse than the style of the dress. Letting down her hair had completely changed the image she habitually presented to the world. Instead of a neat, confining chignon, her loosened hair formed a long, slinky coil down her bare back, its unfastened tresses softening her face. As for the slash of scarlet lipstick Anita had applied—even after several hours and Flavia's liberal use of her napkin over dinner—her lips still looked flushed and beestung.

Full and inviting…

She stared, transfixed. Oh, God—was that what Leon Maranz had been seeing all evening? All through dinner? And now—much worse—after that dreadful, disastrous dance her face had a hectic flush to it. Her pupils were distended, her breathing far too rapid.

This wasn't her! It wasn't! It *wasn't*! What had happened to her? Where had she gone, that restrained, composed female she strove to be when she was summoned to her father's side? Because one thing was glaringly, appallingly clear: she wasn't here any more. She wasn't sitting on this velvet stool, staring wide-eyed at the reflection gazing back at her. It was a different woman—a completely different woman! Alien and strange.

Sensual…

The word formed in her head and she instantly tried to shake it out, as she would a burr on her sleeve. But it wouldn't go. It would only wind itself sinuously around her consciousness, whispering its poison in her ear.

Sensual…

Instantly she rejected the word. It didn't matter. It didn't matter a jot what Leon Maranz could make her feel! She was not going to have anything to do with him! He belonged to the world of her father—a world in which making ever more money was the most important thing, and spending it as flashily and extravagantly as possible the next most important thing. A shallow, empty, superficial world! She belonged somewhere quite different. In the country, at home at Harford, with her grandmother who loved her so much, needed her so much...

Nothing could alter that,

So it was definitely time to put a stop to whatever Leon Maranz had in mind! A complete full stop. Time to send him a quite different message from the one she'd so disastrously given him by dancing with him.

Squaring her shoulders, she scooped up her hair, twisting it fiercely around her fingers until it was pinioned against the nape of her neck. Then, helping herself to some of the complementary hairgrips laid on for guests at the vanity unit, she ruthlessly pinned it into place. A tissue scrubbed repeatedly over her lips dealt with the remnants of Anita's wretched scarlet lipstick.

She got to her feet. Lifted her chin. She had the rest of the evening to get through somehow, but get through it she would—she must. She would refuse point-blank to dance with Leon Maranz again—refuse to do anything other than offer him the barest civility.

She stared at herself. With her hair up, her lips pale once more, she looked almost her normal self. Only the faint, betraying flush of the skin on her cheeks told of her discomfiture.

Unconsciously she felt the unseen pressure of his hand at her waist, hers on his shoulder. For one lingering moment she could *feel* Leon Maranz's touch...

Then, with a sharp little rasp in her throat, she got to her feet and walked out of the powder room.

CHAPTER FOUR

LEON levered his broad shoulders away from the wall that he'd been propping up while Flavia Lassiter hid from him in the Ladies' Room. Now, finally, she had emerged, as he'd known she would have to eventually, and was walking briskly forward. She'd managed to put her hair up again, and the last remnants of the stunning lipstick that had turned her mouth into a tempting curve had disappeared, but nothing could hide the sinuous beauty of her body in the elegant, figure-skimming evening dress.

As he straightened she saw him, and stopped dead. Colour flared in her cheeks and her eyes flashed. Satisfaction knifed through Leon. She could play the chilly ice-maiden all she liked, but she could not hide that physical, visceral response to him. The one she revealed every time he broke through her guard—every time she stopped holding him at bay the way she was so rigidly trying to do.

'There you are,' he said smoothly, reaching for her arm and tucking it into his with a proprietorial air.

Flavia clenched her teeth. How had he done it? How had he gone and helped himself to her like that? Yet again, just as before, she had the choice of either going along with him or tugging away and making a fool of herself in doing so in front of other people. Stiffly, she let him lead her back into the ballroom, back towards their table. Her hopes that her fa-

ther and Anita—anyone at all!—might be there, were dashed.
The table was deserted.

Courteously, Leon Maranz relinquished her in order to
pull out her chair, and stiffly Flavia lowered herself onto it.
Dear God, would this evening never end? Surely her father
and Anita would get off the damn dance floor and come
back? Even the sight of her father fawning over Leon Maranz
and Anita flirting with him would be preferable to having
to sit here like a sour lemon beside him, while he beckoned
to one of the passing waiters to serve fresh coffee and refill
his brandy glass.

Then he relaxed back in his chair, hooking one arm over
the back and crossing one long leg over the other, and turned
his face towards her. Long lashes dipped down over his glinting eyes.

'Your father's girlfriend was wrong,' he informed her. 'You
look as beautiful with your hair up as down. But then—' his
eyes washed over her consideringly, as if he were scrutinising
an Old Master '—you are, of course, quite exceptional. As you
must know.' He reached for his brandy glass and swirled the
contents slowly. Even more slowly, almost contemplatively,
he said, his tone inviting, 'But I am sure there is a great deal
more to you than your exceptional beauty. Tell me about yourself. What do you do when you are not gracing events like
this evening's? Do you have a career?' he enquired.

His gaze levelled on her and she looked away. She did not
want to talk about her grandmother, or her life in Dorset. It
was completely separate from these unwelcome sojourns in
London with her father. Besides, caring for a grandmother
with dementia and single-handedly looking after an eight-
bedroom house and its gardens was hardly a career.

'No,' she said baldly.

Leon frowned slightly. For all her chilly reserve, Flavia
Lassiter had not struck him as unintelligent, and it was un-
usual these days for a woman like her to have no life of her
own. Most society women made a pretence, at least, of having

an occupation of sorts—even if it were little more than a stab at something they considered light and easy, such as interior design. Many, of course, were high-powered businesswomen and career professionals in their own right.

'No?' he echoed.

'No,' Flavia repeated, looking back at him coolly. Let him think what he would of her. She hardly cared, after all. After this evening she would have nothing more to do with him.

Leon's frown deepened. 'You are content, then, merely to be your father's pampered daughter?' he posed.

Flavia could feel her face freezing at the implication.

'Evidently,' she clipped out.

Leon studied her expression. She hadn't liked the imputation, but then, he mused, perhaps few men had actually put it to her that living off her indulgent father's wealth at her age was not something that could be admired. A thought flickered across his mind. If Flavia Lassiter was indeed entirely reliant on her father's wealth for her comfortable lifestyle— her gown, however lacking in 'bling', was clearly a designer number, for instance, and those were definitely high-carat diamonds in her earlobes and in the slender bracelet snaking around her wrist—how would she cope if that wealth were to evaporate? He knew all too well that if he—or another turn-around expert—did not rescue her father it was the very likely outcome of Lassiter's disastrously fragile financial situation.

Does she know how close to the wind her father is? he speculated. If she truly were a pampered princess then it was unlikely she did. Females like that did not trouble themselves over the source of their funding. They took it for granted that the largesse would not stop. Besides... His eyes narrowed infinitesimally. Unlike Lassiter's mistress, she had made no effort to fawn on him. Just the reverse! Had she any realisation of just how essential he was to her father's continued affluence—and therefore her own—she would surely not be so chilly and rejecting of him!

But her frigid demeanour was because she was trying

to deny the effect he was having on her, he reminded himself. She was trying to resist him. That was why she was so determined to give him the cold shoulder. His dark eyes glinted briefly. Did she really not realise that her attitude would merely spur him on?

Her tension now was visible in the stiffness of her spine. Clearly she was wishing him to perdition—but in that he was not going to oblige her. He took a contemplative mouthful of his drink, enjoying the fine bouquet and fiery resonance of the vintage cognac.

'Perhaps you occupy yourself in charity work?' He trailed the suggestion in front of her.

His reward was a daggered glance. 'Of course,' she agreed. 'Attending essential functions like this one. Which as you can see—' her voice was viciously sweet '—I am *so* enjoying.'

Even as she spoke she knew she'd been unacceptably rude. But it was too late to take her unpleasantly sarcastic riposte back now. Too late, she thought with a hollow grip inside her, to do anything at all about Leon Maranz's disastrous, unwanted impact on her except hold him as far at bay as she possibly could! Even if that meant crossing every boundary of social courtesy.

A desperate thought crossed her haunted mind. Perhaps if she were sufficiently rude to him he'd at least back off and leave her alone. Go off and seek a more willing, complaisant woman—goodness knew there were enough of them here tonight! He could have his pick if he wanted. So why, *why* did he have to focus on *her*, for heaven's sake!

I can't cope with this! I can't cope with having this happening to me here, and now. He's part of my father's world, and I have every reason to reject that world—reject anything to do with it! I've got responsibilities and duties that are two hundred miles away which I cannot abandon even if I were to want to—which I don't. So I just don't want this—I don't want this man paying me attention, trying to pull me, trying to get me into bed. Because that, obviously, is what he wants...

Like a guillotine slicing down, she cut off her train of thought. It was far too dangerous. Emotion writhed in her. All she wanted to do was get to her feet and bolt—just get away from the man invading her presence, disquieting and disturbing her, making his impact felt so powerfully and over-whelmingly.

The sudden tightening of his expression showed her that he had not appreciated her sarcasm, and for a moment she felt an impulse to apologise to him. Then she hardened. Making him dislike her was as good a way as any to keep him at a distance. Besides, a resentful voice said in her head, she didn't *want* to be so affected by him. She didn't *want* to have this fluttery quickening of the pulse, this perpetual shimmer of awareness of him. She wanted to be immune to him, to be unaffected by him, completely indifferent to him.

This time tomorrow I'll be back at home—safe.

She made the thought hang in her head, clinging to it. All she had to do was get through the remainder of this wretched evening and she'd be done. Done with Leon Maranz for good!

She reached for her coffee cup and deliberately let her gaze wander out over the ballroom with an expression of boredom on her face.

Beside her, Leon felt his anger snap its jaws.

'Tell me,' he drawled, his voice like a blade, 'what makes you think you have a right to be rude to me?'

Flavia's head swivelled. Words jumbled fiercely in her brain—hot, angry words that she wanted to hurl at him! But she couldn't—couldn't say the words she was burning to throw at him.

What makes you think you can come on to me the way you are? What makes you think you can drag me out on to the dance floor and make me dance with you, invading my body space, making me react to you the way I did? What makes you think you can look at me the way you do—making it ob-vious...blindingly, searingly obvious...what you want?

But she couldn't hurl those words at him. Instead, all she

could do was glare at him stonily, her face tightening, and retreat behind her rigid, icy guard to keep him at bay. Resort again to the unforgivable rudeness that she knew, with a small, shaming part of her brain, that she was handing out to him.

'I don't think anything about you at all, Mr Maranz,' she said, forcing her voice to be cold. 'You're my father's guest, not mine, and I would far rather he did a host's duty by you instead of leaving the task to me.'

Involuntarily her eyes went past him to the dance floor, urgently trying to seek out her wretched father and Anita. Would they get off the floor and come back to their table?

Leon saw her searching gaze. Was that, maybe, what this was all about? Was Alistair Lassiter's idle, pampered daughter sulking because her father paid more attention to his mistress than to her?

He took a mouthful of brandy, studying Flavia's rigid face. 'Are you jealous of Anita?' he ventured.

Again Flavia's gaze snapped to him. *'What?'*

He gave a slight shrug. 'It would not be surprising. Daughters—especially those who are used to being Daddy's darling—are very often extremely possessive of their fathers, and resent them paying attention to any other female. Let alone one as young and glamorous as Anita.'

Flavia could only stare. 'You think I'm jealous of *Anita*?' She could not hide the disbelief in her voice.

'Why not?' Leon replied. 'Your father seems quite…smitten by her.'

Flavia could feel her face icing. 'Anita,' she bit out, 'is a gold-digging piece of work who wouldn't look twice at him if he weren't rich! Every bit of jewellery she's dripping with, every designer number in her vast collection, was paid for by *him*!'

There was scorn in her voice, and she didn't bother to hide it.

Leon's reply was hard. 'You are fortunate, then, that *you* only had to be born your father's daughter to enjoy his wealth.'

At least she had the grace to look discomfited, he saw. His gaze studied her face. Just what *was* Flavia Lassiter's character? On the plus side she seemed unimpressed by his wealth, disdaining to fawn on him, yet she enjoyed the fruits of Alistair Lassiter's largesse and admitted she made no attempt to earn any money for herself, or even busy herself with charity work, which so many women of her type did. And she was perfectly willing to be shamelessly rude to him—was that truly only because she was trying to deny what was so obviously flaring between them?

A dark thought shadowed his mind yet again. Or was it because she saw no necessity to be polite to him because he did not come from the well-bred world she moved in so effortlessly. Because he had started life half a world away in a South American shanty town and come penniless to this country, nothing more than yet another indigent immigrant—someone to look down on and resent, to look through as if he simply did not exist...?

Again he felt the familiar sting of anger inside him, fuelled by an old, old memory of a time when few had seen any need to show him politeness.

He thrust the reflection aside. He would not be haunted by it...by memories of his past...

There was a swirl of glittering purple skirts and Lassiter's mistress, closely followed by Lassiter himself, was approaching the table once more. Anita's face was animated as she hailed Leon.

'There you are! I wondered where you'd got to. *Do* come and dance! Alistair says he's too tired to go on.'

She pouted flirtatiously at Leon and moved to take his hand, but he raised it in negation, giving a slight but definite shake of his head.

'I never dance with another man's woman,' he said.

Anita's pout turned into a displeased moue. Leon could

immediately see she was peeved to be thought of as Lassiter's 'woman', but at the same time she clearly wanted to dance with Leon himself. He could understand why. Alistair Lassiter was not looking his best right now. His face was red and puffed, and there was a line of sweat around his collar. As he sat down heavily he looked his age, and he was running to fat.

Anita perched herself petulantly on the vacant chair next to Leon, then busied herself spending the next ten minutes making up to him shamelessly. Leon could see Lassiter— not liking it, but at the same time he was obviously not keen on objecting to it. Cynically, Leon found himself once again considering whether Lassiter would actually go so far in ingratiating himself with him by not objecting if he took matters even further with his mistress.

Or his daughter…

His eyes slid past Anita's over-made-up face to where Flavia Lassiter was still sitting stiffly, taking small, repetitive sips from her coffee cup, clearly in an attempt to avoid all further conversation. She was pretending she was occupied in staring out across the ballroom, though it was obvious she was paying her surroundings no attention at all.

Except to him. Flavia Lassiter, whatever his uncertainty or speculation as to her disdain for men of lowly foreign origins, was, Leon knew with complete assurance, radiating a totally female awareness of him on all frequencies—she was bristling with it. Once more a grim sense of satisfaction permeated him. She could snub him all she liked, claim whatever that she didn't think of him at all—but she was lying. Lying all the way down her beautiful slender body…

Making some anodyne reply to whatever it was Anita had just said to him, he turned full face to Flavia.

'If events such as this one tonight are not to your taste, what *do* you care to do with your evenings? Parties? Clubbing?' Deliberately he suggested two things that he'd bet she'd loathe.

He could see her start and stiffen visibly as he addressed

her. Presumably she'd thought he'd turned his unwanted attentions to Anita and she was off his unwelcome hook.

As if all too aware of his daughter's intransigence, Alistair Lassiter answered for her. 'Oh, Flavia's a real culture-vulture,' he effused heartily. 'Offer her a Shakespeare play and she's perfectly happy.'

Leon lifted an eyebrow. 'Indeed? And have you seen the current West End production of *Hamlet*?' He directed his question at Flavia.

'No.' The answer was forced from her.

'Then I would be delighted to take you,' came Leon's smooth reply.

'I don't like the lead actor,' Flavia riposted shortly.

'The National has *Twelfth Night* running,' countered Leon.

She looked straight at him. 'I've seen it too often,' she replied, sounding bored.

No way, no *way* was she going to get cornered into going to the theatre with Leon Maranz. Anyway, she reminded herself with relief, this time tomorrow she'd be back home in Dorset.

'The National's production is highly innovative,' Leon came back.

'I prefer traditional interpretations,' Flavia returned dismissively.

She knew she was being ungracious and rude, and hated herself for it, but she had to do whatever was necessary to get Leon Maranz's attention off her. It was like being caught in a searchlight, pinning her down, trying to disarm her to get past her guard, her desperate defences.

It was imperative that she hold him at bay. Now even more so. Her father's ingratiating suggestion about the theatre had sent alarm bells ringing yet again. He evidently wanted her to go out with the man, and the only reason he wanted that must be that he'd decided it would further his ambitions to do lucrative business with Leon Maranz.

I won't be used like that! I won't!

The rejection was vehement, adamant. She had never let

herself be set up by her father in such a way, and she wouldn't start now! Not even with a man she was so attracted to. *That* was why she had to cut Leon Maranz—even if it meant she had to resort to open rudeness the way she was doing. He wouldn't leave her alone, wouldn't accept that she was refusing to have anything to do with him, refusing to give an inch, a centimetre to him.

And if she didn't...

Like a traitor to her resolve, her gaze refocussed, for a fleeting moment, on his face. She could feel her pulse surge treacherously even as she hated herself for succumbing. Feel her eyes flare, her breath quicken.

Why this man?

That was the impossible question. The one she had no answer to. The one that confounded everything.

But it doesn't matter! The cry sounded in her head, silencing the question she could not—would not—answer. It didn't matter why this man? Because the only salient thing about him was that he was all bound up with her father and his endless attempts to use her to his own advantage. And because of that it didn't matter a damn what she thought of Leon Maranz, or what she might otherwise do about the way he looked at her, the way he got under her skin, the way he got past her guard, the way he made her feel. It just didn't matter!

And this evening didn't matter. And it didn't matter that she was being rude to him. It didn't matter that her father was clearly hopping mad at the way she was behaving, and that Anita was throwing dagger-looks at her. Or that Leon Maranz's eyes were resting on her as if he had just lifted a stone and seen something crawl out from underneath it

It just didn't matter...

For a moment sheer, raw misery filled her, intermingled with the self-contempt she could feel flushing through her for the way she was being right now—the way she had been ever since she had realised that it was *this* man her father wanted her to be nice to. He wanted her to accept his company, his attentions, his invitation to go the theatre with him.

Resentment spiked through her misery. Resentment at her father for putting her in this invidious position in the first place, for not giving a damn about her at all and never having done, for not caring about her mother, or her grandmother, or anyone else except himself and what he wanted. Resentment of Leon Maranz, who wanted to do business with a man like her father and who assumed she was nothing more than a pampered, workshy snobbish socialite!

And yet underlying all those layers of resentment was a deeper layer still—resignation. Resignation because with her grandmother to care for any relationship with anyone was impossible…just impossible…

Emotion twisted inside her, like wires around her throat.

'I *adore* the theatre!' Anita's breathless gush was a welcome invasion of her inner turmoil. 'And cabaret especially.' Her eyes widened as if she'd had a sudden idea. 'There's a really good new cabaret club opened recently—it's got rave reviews. How about if we all go on to it now?' She beamed.

'Great idea,' Alistair Lassiter enthused, getting heavily to his feet. 'I think we've done our bit here,' he said portentously, nodding at the charity signage.

Anita stood up eagerly. 'Brilliant!' she breathed, and radiated her fulsome smile at Leon.

Flavia's heart sank. *Oh, no.* To be dragged off to some wretched club—please, no!

But Leon Maranz was shaking his head. 'I've an early start tomorrow,' he said. 'I must be making a move.'

Thank God, Flavia found herself thinking fervently. But the next moment she realised she had been premature—disastrously premature.

'Well, in that case,' her father was saying, holding Anita closely at his side, 'I'd be very grateful if you could see my daughter home safely. You'd be all right with that? I'd worry about her otherwise.'

He spoke with his customary public doting fondness that made Flavia cringe at its falsity. And at the implications of what he'd just asked Leon Maranz to do.

She stood up hastily. 'I'm perfectly capable of getting a taxi,' she said tartly.

But Leon Maranz had got to his feet as well. 'I wouldn't dream of it,' he replied. His voice was smooth, emollient. 'Of course I'll see you home.'

Her father was rubbing his hands. 'Good, good,' he said. 'Well, then, if we're all ready for the off…?'

Stiffly, relieved the ordeal of the charity bash was finally over, but more than dreading the journey back to her father's apartment, Flavia walked briskly from the ballroom. Could she possibly manage to snaffle a taxi immediately outside the hotel and make her getaway?

But getting away from Leon Maranz when he was on the prowl proved impossible. Leon's chauffeur was already holding the door of his waiting car open for her, and she had no recourse but to climb in. Thankfully the interior was huge, and she squeezed herself against the far side of the wide seat, hastily drawing the seat belt over her and fastening it, lest Leon Maranz attempt the office himself. But he had simply thrown himself into the other side of the seat, fastened his own belt, and stretched his long legs out into the spacious well behind the glassed-in driver.

A moment later the limo was pulling out into the late night traffic of Park Lane. It would take a good fifteen to twenty minutes, at best, Flavia knew with sinking heart, to get to Regent's Park.

She wondered whether Leon Maranz was going to attempt any form of conversation with her, but to her relief he merely glanced at her, bestowed a brief, social smile upon her, then took out a mobile phone from his tuxedo and proceeded to make a series of phone calls. All were of a business nature, and Flavia allowed herself the respite of letting her head rest against the smooth, cool leather of the headrest and close her weary eyes.

She didn't want to look at him. Didn't want to see him, long legs stretched out, shirt moulding his broad chest, strong, compelling features animated, as he gave what appeared to be a series of terse instructions to those who were presumably his minions. No, she didn't want to look at him at all. Wanted to blank him out—write him out of her existence.

In a short while I'll be done with him and this whole impossible situation will finally be over! I'll never have to set eyes on him again!

She waited for relief to flood through her—because it must, obviously, at the thought of finally being shot of the man who had caused her nothing but nerve-racking jitteriness all the endlessly long evening.

But it didn't come.

Instead she felt her eyes flick open, her head turn sideways. Her gaze light on the man who had caused her so much torment.

Out of nowhere she felt her pulse jolt, her throat catch. Her eyes fastened to him, to his aquiline profile, to his features cast into stark relief by the street lights as they moved across his face with the car's motion. She wanted to gaze at him, not tear her eyes away. Just go on gazing at him. Drinking him in.

She was never going to see him again...

And suddenly—ridiculously, absurdly, insanely—she knew she didn't *want* never to see him again. Didn't want to know that for the rest of her life the most she would ever see of this man would be if she looked him up on the internet, or saw his photo in the pages of the financial news.

In this enclosed, contained space, with the anonymous driver invisible behind his smoked glass partition, the outer world beyond the tinted windows was shut out. The world that was full of resentment of her father and responsibility for her grandmother. It all seemed suddenly remote, distant. Instead, there was only the cocooning space of the car's interior, a world of its own, closed and intimate. Enclosing herself and the man sitting only a metre away from her, his presence so close it was like a physical pressure on her.

She caught the male scent of him—the faint aroma of brandy, of expensive lightly spiced aftershave. Saw the slight darkening of his jawline, the sable feathering of his hair, the profile of his long dark eyelashes. Everything about him was assailing her senses. She felt faint with it, her breath catching. She clung to the leather strap in the car's interior, her other hand crushing her clutch bag, her breath held in her lungs, and she could not tear her eyes away from him.

As if in slow motion, it seemed to her, he turned his head towards her. Looked back at her full-on, meeting her helpless gaze. Helplessly she saw him halt his call in mid-speech. In slow motion he seemed to cut his call, slide his phone back into his jacket pocket, keeping his attention totally, completely on her.

And she couldn't tear her eyes away—still couldn't. She could feel her eyes flaring, her focus dissolving. Her breath was frozen, and his gaze on her made her feel as she had never felt before...

And then he smiled.

Not a brief, impersonal one as he had before.

A slow, sensual smile.

Personal.

Intimate.

It was as if the whole world had slowed down. The car was at a traffic light and the low, powerful throb of the engine seemed to be vibrating all the way through her, accentuating the slow, heavy throb of her own heartbeat. She felt herself dissolving, melting, kept upright only by the physical power of his gaze levelled on her, holding her like a physical grip, refusing to relinquish her.

He was forcing her to acknowledge him—to acknowledge his power over her. The power of his desire for her...

Of hers for him...

Because that was what it was—she knew it, accepted it. Whatever she might think of this man, she knew that he affected her in a way no other man ever had. In a way that she'd had no idea she *could* be affected. She might resist it, resent it, reject it—but she could feel the potent force of it, feel her susceptibility, her vulnerability. Feel herself, her body, the blood in her veins, answering it. Feel it drawing her...

She sat motionless, her eyes fastened to his, as the low throb of the car's engine vibrated through her consciousness. She was there, in that captive space, the world beyond nothing but a dim blur of noise and discordant lights. All that existed was her—and the man now reaching out his hand, letting his fingers trail slowly down the curve of her cheek, a smile playing about his mouth.

And she let him. Let him smile at her knowingly, intimately. Let him reach for her, touch her. Let his fingers draw softly down the satin of her cheek. Felt a thousand nerve-endings sigh like velvet melting.

Let him curve his hand around the tender nape of her neck, the tips of his fingers shaping her skull. Let him murmur something...she knew not what. Because her gaze was held by his, liquid into liquid, and then his head was bending towards hers, he was taking her mouth with his.

She could not move. Not a muscle. Not a fibre of her being. Her entire being was in the sensation he was creating, the silk of his mouth laving hers.

Her eyes closed, helpless, as his kiss deepened. And she yielded to it—to him—for how could she do otherwise? How could she do anything but let this exquisite, sensuous touch go on and on and on? She arched towards him, yearning towards him, and the pressure of his fingers at her nape strengthened. She felt with a susurration of shock that his other hand was shaping her breast, splaying across it, and it was ripening to his touch, her nipple cresting against his palm. It was the most incredible feeling she had ever felt. Her mouth was opening to his, and all she wanted in all the world was to have him kiss

her, to arch her body towards him and feel it fire with a pleasure so intense she gave a low, insensible moan in her throat.

'I've been waiting for this moment since the first I set
eyes on you...'

His voice was low against her mouth. Husky, but with an
intensity about it that penetrated through all the layers of her
defences just as his touch, his possessing kiss, had penetrated.

For a long, endless moment his eyes entwined with hers,
and she was helpless, utterly helpless, to do anything but let
her gaze sink into his, let the slow, heavy slug of her heart
resonate with his. His eyes held hers, his mouth grazed hers,
his palm cupped her breast...

'Come back with me now—tonight—stay with me.'

The low husk of sensual desire was still in his voice, but
there was another note, too...

Confidence. Assurance.

Assumption.

And suddenly her body was no longer boneless, pliant in
his clasp. She pulled back, pulled away. He reached for her
again, as if to reclaim her, but Flavia stiffened. In an instant
she was the way she had been all evening.

And in the next instant she had reached for the door handle, acting instinctively, urgently. She had to get out! *Now!*

'Flavia!'

She heard her name, but she was gone. Pushing open the
car door, standing momentarily on the road, then in the next
instant registering that the vehicle in the lane beside her was
a taxi with its 'For Hire' light showing. She yanked open the
passenger door and tumbled inside just as the driver, taken by
surprise, started forward when the lights changed to green.

'Regent's Park!' she bit out urgently, and collapsed back
into the seat. Her heart was pounding, her head muzzy with
shock. She closed her eyes.

Dear God, what had she let happen? How—*how* had she
let it happen? How had Leon Maranz gone from ignoring her
and making phone calls to making love to her...?

Kissing me like that—caressing me like that!

She glanced down at her torso. Mortification swept over her—her nipples were still crested, aroused. Compelling, undeniable witness to just what she had done—what she had let him do...

Her body seemed to be fizzing as if champagne were bubbling through it, as if it was still resonating from his kiss, his caress. It seared through her brain so she could still feel the impact of his touch.

I got out just in time—just in time!

It was a mantra that replayed itself for the rest of the night and was still there in the morning. Desperately she tried to find a reason for why Leon Maranz had been able to so precipitately sweep aside her defences the way he had—overwhelm her guard as effortlessly as if she had never raised it in the first place.

He took me by surprise. I didn't stand a chance!

Yes, that was it—that was how it had happened! She'd been holding him at bay all evening—holding down her hopeless reaction to him, her disastrous attraction to him—and it had been so hard to do, so hard to keep fighting it the whole time, with him doing his best to get past her guard, to thaw her frigid defences against him. And then out of nowhere, just as she'd thought him finally distracted by his business calls, she'd stupidly let herself gaze at him, and then he'd sensed her momentary lapse, realised her weakness...and made his move.

Swiftly, expertly, overwhelmingly...

Sweeping away all her resistance. Overpowering her defences as if they were made of cotton wool.

Hot, sensuous memory flooded through her synapses like a warm, seductive wave of sensation, as she replayed those moments in his arms, his mouth exploring hers, his palm shaping her breast...

No! No, she *must not* let herself remember, recall, replay...

Must shut that memory right down, lock it down so that she was no longer haunted by it.

That was what she told herself all that day, on the train journey down to Dorset. She had set her alarm early to get out of the apartment before her father and Anita surfaced, to get to the station and pile herself on to a morning train, to stare sightlessly out of the window as she passed the time *not* thinking, *not* remembering...

Only rationalising. Ruthlessly, remorselessly, rigorously.

I met a man. A man like I've never met before. And for some inexplicable and irrational reason he had an effect on me no other man has ever had. Which is ridiculous, because he's nothing like any man I've ever been out with! And it's impossible even to contemplate anything with him! He belongs to my father's world and I want nothing to do with it—and even if he didn't I still can't have anything at all to do with him, because my place is with my grandmother. I have an indelible responsibility for her, and nothing on earth can change that. Nothing.

And if he did sweep past my defences last night, then I must take that as even stronger evidence that I should and can and must have absolutely nothing more to do with him! Because he's made it clear—crystal clear!—that he'd sweep me off to bed as well!

Would she have gone with him?

That was the stark, unanswerable question that hung in her head. He had assumed she would—she'd heard it in his voice, heard that note of confidence, of assurance. Of course, since she'd melted in his arms in the back of his limo, she would melt all over him in bed straight away!

And you would have, too...

The whispering, treacherous thought wound into her brain and found an echo in her treacherous flesh...which quickened at the thought. Her pulse was insistent, a sensual, shimmering tremor quivering through her body. A vision leapt in her mind: herself entwined with him, laid upon a wide, waiting bed, and his dark sloe eyes burning into her as he possessed himself of her with mouth and hands and all his strong, lean body...

But it was a vision—only that. Nothing more. Not real, not actual—and it never could be, never would be.

She swallowed, forcing herself to focus on the passing landscape beyond the windows of the train. All around her the wide English countryside spread to the horizon. Fields and hedges and woods and little houses, all flashing past. She was going home. She was going back to her grandmother and *that* was her reality. Only that.

A man who could melt her with a single glance of his dark, dark eyes was *nothing* to do with her.

Nothing.

She went on staring sightlessly.

Inside her, a little pool of bleakness formed.

CHAPTER FIVE

Leon sat back impassively in the large leather chair in his London office. Alistair Lassiter was talking at him. He'd been talking at him for the last twenty minutes, and Leon had stopped listening after the first ten. He'd heard all he needed to know. The man was getting desperate. That much was screamingly obvious. Leon had been well aware of the financial precariousness of the Lassiter organisation, but now—whether he realised it or not, and Leon suspected he didn't—Alistair Lassiter had shown him that there were no white knights in the offing to save his sorry, extravagant skin.

All that was left for Leon to decide was whether he would do so.

But that wasn't what was currently occupying his mind.

It wasn't Alistair Lassiter's business affairs that were pre-occupying him. It was his daughter. Thoughts about her were going round and round in succession.

Talk about conflicted...

After their final barbed exchange at the charity function, with Flavia Lassiter doing her damnedest to make him think her rude and stuck up to the point where he was almost ready to wash his hands of her, he'd then completely reversed his decision while taking her home! She'd only had to look at him the way she had, so close to him in the dim, closeted privacy of the car. When she'd met his gaze full-on, drowning in his eyes, every reservation about her had been submerged in an overwhelming desire to do just what he had—sweep her into his arms and kiss her....

And it had been a disaster! Oh, not the kiss—that had been a sensual white-out!—but the timing couldn't have been worse.

I rushed her.

That was the accusation that was staring him in the face. He'd rushed her—and panicked her. And she'd bolted.

It was too much, too soon. She couldn't handle it, couldn't accept it—not so suddenly.

Her rudeness to him he could now see was obviously her attempt to fight their attraction to each other, which she just couldn't cope with—at least not yet. Hence her precipitate reaction to him when he'd kissed her. Self-accusation stabbed again. He'd indulged his own desires at her expense, and the result had been she'd bolted.

He took a steadying breath—OK, so he'd mishandled the situation, acted like an impulsive teenager instead of an experienced man who should have read the situation more adroitly, but that kiss had been proof to both of them of just how powerfully attracted they were to each other. She would find that kiss as impossible to forget as he did.

Resolution replaced his berating of himself. All he had to do now was consider the best way of taking the situation forward to the conclusion that was, he knew with every atom in his body, as inevitable as day following night. All he had to do was find the right way to woo her.

Leon's eyes refocussed on Lassiter, glinting in impatience—he would far rather be focussing on Lassiter's daughter, undoing the damage his kiss had done, not listening to her father extol the wonderful 'investment opportunity' of saving his company. A frown creased Leon's brow minutely. How would Flavia react if he decided *not* to bail out her father? Would she still want anything to do with him? A disquieting memory of their conversation last night about how she seemed content to accept her father's financial support wormed its

way into her head. Impatiently, he thrust it aside. To many
women of her background acting as a social hostess was occupation enough. It was the way they'd been brought up.

What will she do if her father goes under?

The question hovered in his head, uncomfortable and troubling.

With sudden decision he shifted in his seat and flexed his
shoulders. He wasn't prepared to take the risk that Flavia
Lassiter would want to have anything more to do with him at
all if she knew he'd chosen to let her father go down the drain.
So he'd bail out Lassiter—but on his own terms.

He held up a hand, interrupting Alistair Lassiter's self-
justifying peroration.

'You've made your case. I'm interested. But there are conditions. I'll want equity, executive control, and my own finance man in place to authorise future spending. And you'll
have to pull out of some of your African deals—the ones in
Luranda—I don't do business with dictators, however much
they lavish their country's foreign aid revenues and natural
resources on me.'

Lassiter's face reddened. 'Equity? I was looking more at
lines of credit—'

Leon shook his head. 'I always insist on equity,' he spelt
out.

Lassiter promptly took another tack instead. 'You can't
be serious about pulling out of Luranda? The profit margins
are massive!'

'At the expense of the country's benighted people,' Leon
retorted.

'Lurandans are notoriously lazy and feckless—like all too
many in the Third World,' Lassiter blustered.

Leon levelled a cold gaze on him. 'Desperate and ex-
ploited,' he said.

'Yes, well…as long as they stay in the Third World and
don't keep trying to get here and leech off us—' started
Lassiter, then stopped abruptly.

'You were saying?' Leon queried. The coldness in his eyes was sending a message even Lassiter could read.

'Well, obviously the enterprising ones can make a go of things—just like you have.' Lassiter was back to blustering again.

'But those like me,' Leon pursued, 'would far prefer to be able to make a go of things in their *own* countries. Which is seldom possible when outside money is propping up their corrupt, exploitative and grossly economically inefficient government for its own benefit. Which is why,' he spelt out, 'Maranz Finance only ever makes investments in such countries direct at ground level, and retains control over them to ensure middlemen and government officials can't take the profit away from those who do the actual work.'

He got to his feet. He wasn't about to debate the issue. Those were the terms of his involvement, and if Alistair Lassiter didn't like them he could walk. But he wouldn't, Leon knew. He had no choice. There were no other white knights in the offing, and if Lassiter wanted to save his company and, more importantly for him, Leon thought cynically, his fortune, then he'd have to swallow his self-importance and accept the deal on the table.

However, there was no point rubbing the guy's nose in it—Lassiter might prove a pain to work with if he felt too put down by Leon. Maybe it was time to back off and lighten the atmosphere.

It was obvious that Lassiter liked to do business via socialising, and although Leon had had quite enough of *his* company, the reverse was true of his daughter. Knowing he was keen on his daughter would definitely sweeten the atmosphere.

'Now,' he said, his voice warming as he walked around the desk, 'with our business discussion out of the way, I wanted to thank you for a most enjoyable evening last night. However, I don't believe I have the phone number of your London apartment. I'd like to ask your daughter out to dinner tonight.'

A quiet dinner—a chance to make amends for his behaviour the night before, a chance to get to know Flavia properly, woo her properly. That was what he was after now.

He paused expectantly by Alistair Lassiter, who got to his feet. But to his surprise, instead of being immediately and eagerly forthcoming with the number, the man looked discomfited.

'Ah, yes, Flavia—of course,' the man floundered. 'Yes, yes—the thing is she's gone out of town—left this morning—prior engagement, so she told me.'

Leon stilled. 'She's not in London?'

'Er…as it happens, no,' corroborated Lassiter.

'When is she planning to return?' Leon asked.

His voice was even, unemotional. But inside his emotions were streaming through him. He'd thought, when she'd jumped ship into that taxi, it had only been the spur of the moment, that she'd just panicked, been overwhelmed by what had happened between them, and had needed some space to come to terms with it. But actually leaving town?

'And,' he went on, keeping his voice deliberately cool through the emotion spiking in him, 'where has she gone?'

'The thing is, I'm not really sure.' Lassiter attempted to sound nonchalant, and failed. 'You know these days they're so independent.'

'Any ideas?' Leon wasn't about to let him off the hook. 'Where do her friends live?'

'Oh—all over, really. I couldn't say. Could be anywhere.'

Leon decided to cut to the chase. 'OK, give me her mobile number and I'll find her myself.'

'Er—yes, of course. The thing is though…um…she may not answer it.'

'I'll take my chances,' said Leon implacably.

Wherever she'd run to, he would find her. He'd screwed up with her and he had to fix it.

He wanted her too much not to.

Far, far too much.

'Hello, Gran, darling.' Flavia leant over her grandmother's bed and kissed her cheek tenderly. She'd only just arrived from the station, but there was no point telling her grandmother that. It would not register. 'Mrs S says you've had a very good lunch,' she said encouragingly. 'Mashed potatoes, peas and plaice.'

Her grandmother looked at her uncertainly, and her thin fingers picked at the turned-down sheet across her torso. Pain shafted through Flavia. It hurt so much to see her once vibrant grandmother so frail, so lost in the mist of her own mind.

'Plaice is your favourite type of fish,' she said.

But her grandmother's gaze had drifted away, settling on some indeterminate point ahead of her. Flavia lifted her veined hand, and squeezed it gently, looking down at her grandmother, lying there in her double bed—the same bed she'd slept in for over fifty years, since coming to Harford as a young bride. Her heart contracted as she felt the pity of it all. Yet there was a kind of mercy in it, too, she knew. It had been the death of Flavia's grandfather that had first set her off on this journey into a darkening land. Had she lost the will to take part in life once the man she had lived with and loved for so long, had gone?

Flavia smiled sadly as she left the room. What would it be like to love a man so much that you no longer wanted to live once he was not at your side any more? To her it was unimaginable. She'd never been in love, fond though she'd been of former boyfriends. There had never been any great depth of feeling for them, and whilst she'd found them attractive there had never been anyone to arouse a storm of passion in her breast.

Of desire.

Her expression changed, and the memory she'd been banning since getting back home leapt vividly in her head. Instantly, helplessly, she was back in Leon Maranz's arms...

Passion and soft, sensual arousal that teased and laved and melted, so that the breath quickened, the pulse surged, and the body arched and yearned towards the source of it. His mouth warm on hers, pliant and tasting, taking hers with his, and heat starting to beat up through her body, like a dissolving glow...

No! With sheer effort, she dragged her mind away. It was madness to let herself remember. She had spent the whole train journey down to Dorset trying to shut it out, trying not to let it play over and over again in her mind like some impossible video loop she could not turn off.

But now, safely back at Harford, with her grandmother again—back in her real life, a cosmos away from her father's world and the darkly dangerous man who moved therein—surely she was safe from that disastrous memory? If she could just put it completely behind her, write it off as some appalling, unforgivable misjudgement, a lapse that she must never think of again.

This—here, now—was her real life.

As she walked downstairs, heading for the kitchen, she made herself look about her, see the safe, familiar walls enclosing her, the safe, familiar paintings, the safe, familiar furniture and décor, the same now as it had been all through her childhood. Her home, her grandmother's home—her safe place to be.

She went through into the large stone-flagged kitchen with its huge, ancient Aga and massive scrubbed wooden table centre stage, and repeated the reassuring litany of familiarity and safety. Everything here was as it had always been, and that was what she wanted.

She busied herself making her grandmother's supper—just something light: soup and scrambled eggs on toast and a mashed banana. She would eat the same, in her grandmother's bedroom, once she'd bade goodbye and thanks to the stalwart Mrs S, and paid her for her extra time. Then, when her grandmother had settled for the night and slipped over into sleep, she would settle down in the armchair by the table by the window, with a low-lit lamp for light, and read. The only sound would be that of her grandmother's gentle breaths and the occasional hooting of an owl outside, sweeping soundlessly over the gardens. Later she would make herself a cup of tea, read a little longer, then head for bed herself, leaving the door to the landing open so she would hear if her grandmother proved restless in the night.

It was a long-familiar routine. Just as the routines of the daytime were. Getting her grandmother up, helping her downstairs, settling her in the sunny drawing room while she got on with the housework, and then, after lunch, if the weather were clement, opening the French windows to the gardens and getting some gardening done while keeping an eye on her grandmother at the same time.

Sometimes the occasional visitor would come and pay a call on her grandmother, though the conversation was always with Flavia herself, and one of the district nurses or healthcare workers would make a daily phone call to check on things. Twice a week they would come and look after her grandmother while Flavia drove into the nearby market town to buy groceries and any other necessary shopping.

A familiar, routine way of life. Quiet, safe, and very dear to her.

Too safe, too quiet...?

The disquieting thought flickered through her synapses. Restlessly she pushed it aside. Yes, of course anyone might tell her that living quietly in the country as she did, looking after an elderly, frail grandparent, with nothing else in her life at all but that and housework and gardening, was no life for a woman in her twenties! But there was nothing she could do about it. Nothing she *wanted* to do about it.

Even as she formed the thought memory licked again, and

it was as if she could feel the pressure of his mouth on hers, feel the surging of her body, her breast straining against the sensuous palm of his hand shaping her. Involuntarily she felt her breasts tightening.

No! It was no good—no good at all letting herself think about that kiss, that embrace. It had been a terrible mistake, a disastrous weakening of her resolve, yielding to an impulse that was impossible—*impossible*! She'd gone through all the reasons why it had been impossible—what was the point of reiterating them? She was home now. Home and safe...

Gratitude filled her that she was safely back here again, where she loved to be, and where the only person in the world who loved her was. The *only* person she loved.

Her heart tightened. Seeing her grandmother again after a space of several days had brought home to her just how much frailer she was, how her body was steadily giving up the will to stay alive, how she was drifting ever deeper into the mists that were calling her.

How long would it be before she slipped away entirely? Body as well as mind? The doctor, on his regular visits to check her over, always said that it was impossible to know for sure, but Flavia knew that now it really could not be that long. Months, perhaps? If that? Or would she still be here this time next year?

Resolutely she put aside such pointless speculation. All that was important—essential—was that her grandmother would live out her days here, at Harford, with her beloved granddaughter, and that was that. Nothing could change that, and Flavia would allow nothing to endanger it.

Her thoughts moved on, becoming more troubled. Here in the familiar surroundings of Harford's comfortably old-fashioned kitchen, as she cracked eggs into a bowl and set the soup to heat, it was as if she had never been away. But she had—and this latest compulsory visit to London had been incredibly disturbing. She could use all the mental discipline she liked to try and shut out what had happened, but it could not shut out that it *had* happened. That she had encountered such a man as Leon Maranz—and that he had had such a devastating impact on her.

And she had fallen into his arms...

But I ran! I ran just in time! Got back here.

Apprehension webbed about her. What if she had to encounter him again, when her father next summoned her? If her father were going to do business with him she might well have to see him again.

I can't! I can't risk seeing him again—I just can't!

That disastrous, debilitating embrace in his limo had shown her just how terrifyingly vulnerable she was to the man. If she had to socialise with him again, and if he still wanted to amuse himself with her, would she find the strength to resist his advances?

Bitterly, she knew the truth.

It would be impossible.

Even now, two hundred miles away from him, she could feel his power dominating her memory if she for a single moment allowed him in. He would overwhelm her, invade her sanctuary here. And she couldn't allow it—she just couldn't! She could never allow herself to become involved with Leon Maranz—however much he drew her with his dark, disturbing sensuality.

Resolve filled her. There *was* a way to avoid it—a way to ensure that she never had to go into that world again, a way to ensure that her father had no power to summon her like a puppet whose strings he could jerk whenever she wanted. Her face shadowed. It was an option she had considered before and turned down. Harford was not hers, and nor were any of its contents. Yet she had power of attorney for her grandmother, so legally she was free to do what she wanted with her grandmother's possessions.

Up till now she had always refused to do anything other than sell the barest minimum to keep them both here at Harford. But to pay off the thousands of pounds of debt her father kept dangling over her head in order to ensure her compliance with his determination to use her when it suited him she would, she knew with a heavy heart, have to sell some of the more valuable antiques that were left, deeply reluctant though she was to do so.

The next morning, before she could change her mind, she phoned the auction house that was located in the county town, and arranged for one of their valuers to call that afternoon. When he came he identified several items—furniture and silver, and a landscape painting by a well-known Victorian watercolourist—that he expected to sell for the amount of money she would need to pay back her father, but it was still with that heavy heart that she committed them to the sale-room's next auction.

Guilt continued to pluck at her. But by early evening, however, she knew she had made the right decision. She had started to receive messages on the landline answer-machine from her father.

She'd been aware he'd been phoning and texting on her mobile, which she'd ignored, and now she did the same to the landline messages he left, irately ordering her to phone him back. The latest, however, which she heard as she came down from her grandmother's room in the early evening, stopped her in her tracks.

'Leon Maranz is trying to get in touch with you. He's complaining to me that you aren't returning his calls on your mobile. Damn well answer them, girl—he's not someone I want annoyed! What the *hell* do you think you're playing at? Just phone him back!'

Her father's angry voice was cut off, and Flavia was left staring at the handset in its cradle on the table by the front door. Cold flushed through her.

Then heat.

Then, jerkily, she snatched up the phone and hit the 'message delete' button.

But she could not delete the memory of what her father had said.

Leon Maranz was trying to get in touch with her.

Emotion spiked through her. It was dismay—of course it was dismay! How could it be anything else? This was exactly why she had fled London! Just as she'd dreaded, he'd taken that damn episode in his limo as some kind of encouragement! And now he wanted more.

Into her mind's eye leapt a vivid imprint of his strong, saturnine face, the dark, heavy-lidded eyes levelled at her. Their message crystal clear. As if she had lifted a floodgate memory poured into her head, and for one long, endless moment she was back in the limo, gazing helplessly at him as with the lean, casual power of a predator he moved in on her to take his fill of her...

She dropped the phone back in its cradle, realising her hand was shaking.

Whatever it took—*whatever* it took—she would never go back to London—never again put herself in the path of Leon Maranz. She would sell those antiques, pay back her father and never again be used and manipulated by him. Never again be trailed by him like alluring bait in front of the men he wanted to do business with.

Even if that man were Leon Maranz.

Especially if that man were Leon Maranz.

CHAPTER SIX

LEON dropped his phone on his desk and threw himself moodily back in his chair.

Were the hell *was* she? Flavia Lassiter had disappeared off the face of the earth. Her father had admitted he had no idea where she was, speculating only that she must be staying with friends, and her mobile was perpetually on voicemail, his texts unreturned. He glared stormily ahead of him across the vast expanse of his office.

Frustration bit at him. OK, so he'd been an idiot, pouncing on her like that, and he'd obviously spooked her big-time. But he was trying to make amends now. Yet how could he do that if she was running shy of him the way she was now?

Was there someone else in her life? If there were, all she had to do was tell him—not bolt and hide the way she had! The poisoning suspicion crawled into his head yet again. Or was it that Flavia Lassiter was not hiding from him because he'd scared her off, but because she had no intention of having anything to do with someone who was not from her own gilded background—who'd made his own painful way up from penury, a no-name immigrant without breeding or class…?

His eyes darkened as he felt once more the suspicion and resentment that her dismissive attitude had first spiked in him. Was that why Flavia Lassiter had gone to ground? Because she wanted nothing to do with a man like him, born and raised in a South American shanty town?

For a moment emotion swirled within him, dark and turbulent. Then, abruptly, he reached for the phone on his desk again. If Flavia Lassiter thought herself above the world he came from, well, he didn't—and he would remind himself of that right now. Remind himself that, for all the glittering riches of the world he lived in here in Europe—the one Flavia Lassiter had been born into and took for granted—back across the Atlantic, in the vast southern hemisphere, teemed millions just like him, living the way he'd once lived. Wanting only a chance, a hope, a stepping stone to a better life, a better future. And to get that future they would work every bit as hard as he had done—harder. All they needed was that first, vital step on their way.

Which was where *he* came in.

He punched through to his PA in the outer office. An impromptu visit would put his fixation with Flavia into perspective—remind him of his roots, of what his wealth had made possible. Values infinitely more essential than those the Lassiters held dear.

'Book me on a transatlantic flight this afternoon—first available carrier. I'll need all the *pro bono* project files updated, and have the local project managers on standby. Tell them to get their latest proposals ready for me to look over—and alert Maranz Microloans I'll want to see their books, plus take in some site visits.'

'What about your appointments today, Mr Maranz?' his PA enquired dutifully. 'Mr Lassiter has phoned twice this morning to check the deal's still on.'

Leon's mouth tightened. Lassiter was trying to hustle him, hoping to change the terms of the deal in his favour. It would be no bad thing to let him sweat for a while—show the man that his terms were non-negotiable.

'Tell him it's postponed,' he said tersely.

'Till when?'

'Till I get back to London—and, no, I don't know when that will be. Next week some time. Maybe later. I'll let you know.' He disconnected. He didn't want a discussion or a debate. He didn't want anything right now except to clear his London desk this morning and head far, far away.

A change of perspective was what he needed. It might help take his mind off the woman who was frustrating the hell out of him.

Flavia was in the garden, dead-heading one of the rows of hydrangeas just beyond the open French windows leading into the drawing room. Her grandmother was in an armchair by the window, a rug over her lap, looking out at her. There was no expression in her face, but her eyes went to Flavia from time to time, and Flavia would pause and chat to her, as if she could really take in what she was saying.

'There's a lot of new growth coming through,' she was saying cheerfully. 'I think I'm going to need to do some watering, too—it's been so dry today. Mind you, if it does stay dry I can get the lawn mown tomorrow. It's looking quite long already.'

She chattered on, determinedly cheerful—as much, she thought with a hollow feeling, to keep her own spirits up as in an attempt to do the same with her grandmother.

It was one thing to know with her head that she absolutely must not have anything more to do with Leon Maranz.

It was quite another thing to accept it.

This is my world, here.

She looked about her. It was a beautiful day, and Flavia could feel her spirits respond to the uplifting sight of Harford's extensive gardens. The lawn was framed by shrubberies, and fronted by a wide herbaceous border. It was a lot to keep up single-handedly, as Flavia did, but it was a labour of love.

Just as caring for her grandmother was a labour of love.

She glanced back, her smile deepening, but there was sadness in it, too, as she looked at her grandmother. She seemed so small and frail and vulnerable, sitting there so still in her chair. As if she were already living in another world.

But she was safe here—safe in the home she had known for over half a century—and this was where she would end her days, with her granddaughter at her side. Nothing would change Flavia's mind on that. If it meant putting her own life on hold—well, so be it. It was a gift she would gladly give her grandmother.

She stretched her shoulders and resumed her clipping, dropping the dried dead heads of the hydrangea into a willow basket. As she got stuck in to her task again she picked up the sound of a vehicle approaching by the front drive. Murmuring to her grandmother, she went in through the French windows and out into the front hall just as the doorbell rang. Opening it, she saw it was the postman.

'Special Delivery,' he said, holding out a pad for her to sign.

She did so, and took the large thick envelope wonderingly, bidding the postman goodbye and shutting the door. She stared at the envelope a moment. It had been franked, but there was a name on the frank she could not read. It was addressed to her—a typed label. Junk mail? Surely not, she reasoned, if it was a special delivery.

She started back to the drawing room, opening the envelope with her fingernail and extracting the contents. Thick folded paper—some kind of document beneath a letter. Frowning in puzzlement, she started reading.

It was from a firm of City solicitors—one she'd never heard of.

As she read, the blood started to congeal in her veins. With shaking hands she dropped the letter on the sofa and sank down beside it on wobbly legs, her eyes burning into the documents. Sickness filled her.

Then, abruptly, she leapt to her feet, seized up the letter, and plunged into the room her grandfather had used as his study. She picked up the phone. Her hands were shaking, the sickness like acid in her stomach, and she could hardly dial the number she knew she had to call.

Her father took her call—as if he were expecting it.

'So,' he said, 'I've finally got your attention, have I? About bloody time!'

Flavia's teeth were gritted. 'What the *hell* have you sent me?' she demanded.

Her father's voice sounded unmoved by her agitation. 'Isn't it clear enough? It's what it says it is—a loan agreement. Plus a note of the accumulated interest since the loan was made.'

'But *when*—when did this happen?' Flavia tried to keep the panic out of her voice and failed.

'It was after your grandad snuffed it. Your gran was worried about money—funeral expenses, legal fees, house repairs, utility bills, all sorts of things. She'd never had to cope with all that stuff. So...'

He paused, and there was an unholy note in his voice. Flavia could hear it, with a hollowing of her insides.

'I offered to help out. Tide her over, so to speak. 'Course, I had to make a bit of profit out of it, didn't I? So maybe the interest rate *was* a bit more than the bank would have charged. But then your gran wouldn't have wanted anyone to know she was borrowing money, would she? Bit *infra dig*, don't you know?' Her ruthlessly mimicked an upper-class accent. 'Whereas having your own son-in-law lend a hand—and some filthy lucre—was quite different!'

Flavia's jaw clenched. Yes, *different*, all right! Though the principle sum loaned had been high, the ruinous, outrageous rate of interest her poor bewildered grandmother had agreed to made the total repayments monstrous! She was still reeling, heaving with shock and sickness. She stared again at the solicitor's letter setting out the total amount currently owed. Dear God—this wasn't a question of selling a few antiques to raise a few thousand. This was ten, twenty times more! A fortune!

Her mind raced frantically. She *had* to pay that terrifying debt off! It was mounting daily, and it was hideous—hideous! But there was only one way to do it. Borrow money to pay it off.

She swallowed, her hand gripping the phone like a vice. 'I'll get it repaid,' she said grimly. 'I'll raise a mortgage on Harford and settle the debt that way!'

How she would pay the mortgage off was something she'd cope with later—right now the only priority was to stop her father's rip-off loan increasing even more, even faster.

Her father gave a laugh. It raised hairs on the back of her neck.

'You haven't got time. The next letter you get from me will be a foreclosure.'

'What?'

'Didn't you read the loan agreement? The loan is secured against Harford, and I can demand repayment at any time. Which means—' there was a fat, satisfied note in his voice that made Flavia want to scream '—I can force a sale whenever I want. Like…tomorrow.'

There was silence. Absolute silence. Flavia could not speak, could not think. Could only stand clutching the phone, swaying with shock, disbelief and horror.

Into the silence, her father spoke.

'It doesn't have to be this way, Flavia. It can be a whole lot easier. In fact—' a new note entered his voice, which made her flesh crawl '—it should be very enjoyable for you—that's what Anita says, and she knows about these things. She's very envious of you.'

Through her pounding heartbeat, Flavia spoke. 'What… what do you mean?'

Her father gave another laugh. Fat and satisfied.

'You've made a conquest,' he informed her. 'Leon Maranz has taken a shine to you—he's keen to get in touch. The only problem is—' Flavia could hear her father's voice ice with anger '—*you* are refusing to play ball!'

Colour flared out along Flavia's cheeks. 'I don't want anything to do with Leon Maranz!'

'Tough!' retorted her father. 'He wants you, and right now anything Leon Maranz wants and I can get him he gets.'

Flavia's chest heaved. 'If you think for a single moment that I—'

Her father cut her off. 'What I *think* is that you will pack your bags and take the first train to London tomorrow morning. And you *will* get in touch with Leon Maranz, and you *will* be very, very nice to him. *Do you understand me*?'

There was ice in Flavia's veins. Ice in her voice. 'What *exactly* do you mean by "nice"?'

Her answer was a coarse, impatient sound. 'Oh, for God's sake—do you want diagrams? You're not a nun—even if you try and dress like one! Though God knows it seems to have turned *him* on, so I guess I can be grateful for that. Maybe he's so spoilt by having stunners all over him that he wants a change? Who cares why? So long as it's you he wants, it's you, my girl, that he's going to get!'

She was gripping the phone so hard she thought it must shatter beneath her hands.

'You want,' she said slowly, each word forced from her, 'to pimp me out to a man you're doing business with?'

Her voice seemed to come from very far away. Horror, disgust and loathing were rising like vomit in her throat. Her father—her own father—was doing this to her...

How can he be this vile—how?

But it didn't matter how. She knew what he was—had known it all her life. Had known all her life that her father did not love her, cared absolutely nothing for her, saw her only as someone to be used...exploited.

Pimped.

Her father was speaking again, and she forced herself to listen. His voice sounded angry now.

'Let me spell out some home truths to you, my girl! This recession has played bloody havoc with me! Right now I need to keep Leon Maranz happy, any damn way he wants, because he's all that stands between me and being totally wiped out! Got it? He's a turnaround merchant—invests in hard-hit companies and pulls them through. Why the *hell* else do you think I'm all over the man? I wouldn't give him the time of day if I didn't need him! Some bloody foreigner lording it over me!'

Instinctively Flavia flinched at the offensive term.

'And you want to pimp me out to him—' scorn was acid in her voice '—just to save your skin.'

Her father gave a derisive, mocking laugh. 'Little Miss Pure and Virtuous? Is that it? Well, you can be as bloody pure and virtuous as you like when you and your senile old bat of a grandmother are out on the streets! Because I promise you—' his voice congealed the breath in her lungs as he spoke '—if you don't play ball and make sure Leon Maranz gets everything he wants from you, I'll rip Harford from you. It'll be on the market this week. So what's it to be? It's make your mind up time.'

Slowly, very slowly, Flavia looked at the documents lying on her grandfather's desk. Saw the zeroes blur, and then re-form. Felt acid leach into her stomach, cold inch down her spine.

Slowly, very slowly, she gave him her answer.

The team of project directors seated around the table were setting out their next round of *pro bono* proposals for funding. Leon knew he should be paying more attention, but his mind was distracted. Focussed elsewhere.

It had been for days now. Focussed on the mobile phone in his jacket pocket. Whenever it rang he was aware of a distinct jolt of expectation and hope. Would it finally, this time, be Flavia Lassiter returning his calls?

But it never was.

He'd hoped that leaving London would stop him being constantly on the alert for her, but here he was on the point of heading back east across the Atlantic and he was just as frustrated by her silence as ever. He'd tried accepting that she just didn't want to know, tried putting her out of his mind, even tried looking out for another woman to take his mind off Flavia Lassiter.

But even the famed beauty of South American womanhood had failed to beguile him. The more he'd tried to be beguiled, the less he had been. The more he'd kept seeing Flavia in his mind's eye, feeling her lips beneath his in his memory, the pliant softness of her body in his embrace...

It was infuriating. It was exasperating. It was unnerving.

I'm becoming obsessed...

The unwelcome notion played in his head, disturbing and disquieting. He tried to rationalise it away, reminding himself that up till now he'd never had to face female rejection—that was why he was reacting so badly to Flavia doing it. But he could rationalise it all he wanted—what he couldn't do was expunge her from his memory or cease to want her.

They'd reached the end of the proposals, and he realised he must make the appropriate answers. Forcing his mind to focus on the subject in hand, he found himself simply giving blanket approval to everything. And why not? he reasoned impatiently. His team were first class, reliable and hardworking, with excellent judgement—it was why he'd picked them in the first place. So their proposals would be fine. He need not check them. Instead he would do what he'd been itching to do all through the meeting. Check his incoming texts.

Dismissing his team with a smile and an expression of appreciation and encouragement, he slid out his phone and hungrily skimmed down the messages.

As he reached the last one he stilled completely. Not a muscle moved in him. For a moment the brief text blurred in his vision, then cleared again.

Sorry I was out of range—FL.

That was all it said—but it was enough. More than enough. For one long moment he simply stared, as if the message might be a mirage. Then, tamping down the emotion that had sprung forcefully inside him, he texted back. A message just as simple—but all he needed to say.

Have dinner with me tomorrow night.

As he hit 'send', his nerves felt strung out like wires. Then, with a total sense of all tension snapping, he saw the brief two-letter reply that told him everything he'd been waiting so long to hear.

OK

It was all he wanted.

Everything he wanted.

Without further hesitation he set off for the airport. He could not be back in London soon enough…

CHAPTER SEVEN

FLAVIA sat on the bed in her bedroom in her father's Regent's Park apartment. Once again she had left her grandmother in the care of Mrs Stephens. Once again she had made the train journey back to London.

A journey that had always been an ordeal for her.

But never like this…

Her hands were clenched in her lap and she felt cold all through her body, despite the warmth of the evening.

She hated her father with all her being for what he was forcing her to do.

Because there was no way she could defy him. That was what was so appalling. She had been over and over and over it in her head, round and round and round. It had occupied her like a hideous monster. She had phoned her grandmother's solicitors the moment he had rung off but, as her father had sneeringly warned her, they knew nothing about the massive loan her grandmother had so rashly, dangerously accepted from her father. Any small hope that he might be bluffing—though really she had known from his air of triumph that he was not—had been swept away the next morning when, after a churning, sleepless night, a car had drawn up at Harford and a slick-looking estate agent from a non-local firm had emerged, primed to inspect the house and value it for 'immediate sale', as he'd oleaginously declared. He'd been closely followed by a courier who had delivered an ominous packet with the name of her father's city solicitor's name on it. Filled with dread she'd opened it, and there it was—a foreclosure notice.

For twenty-four hours Flavia had wrestled with the nightmare, taking all the documents in to the local solicitors in a hope against hope that there might be something flawed about them. But, as her father had told her, there was nothing they could do. Nothing at all. He could take Harford from her and her grandmother any time he wanted.

Any time at all…

Unless she did what he was demanding of her…

Anguish filled her. Not just because she was having to face up to just how monstrously selfish her father truly was, how utterly uncaring of her, but because of more than that.

Into her head came the image she was trying not to let in. The lean, disturbing face of Leon Maranz, who had had such a dangerous, powerful impact on her. An impact she had had to deny, reject. Her stomach hollowed. But now she was being forced to accept it after all.

Her hands twisted in her lap. She hated herself for what she was doing.

But she was going to do it anyway. She was going to go out to dinner with Leon Maranz, accept the situation—accept anything and everything he wanted of her.

She swallowed heavily, then, a moment later jumped. It was the internal phone. The concierge was calling up to tell her that her car had arrived. For a long moment she did not move. Then, slowly, very slowly, she stood up and left the apartment.

Walking on leaden feet.

Leon had chosen the restaurant with care. He wanted Flavia to like it—to feel comfortable there. It was the antithesis of anywhere Alistair Lassiter and his flashy girlfriend would choose. They would want somewhere fashionable, where people went to see and be seen. This place was totally different.

He glanced around with a sense of having chosen well. The restaurant was an eighteenth-century town house in Mayfair that prided itself on retaining and recreating as much of the ambience of that period as possible. All the furniture was antique, and the panelled walls were hung with old paintings and portraits. The original sash windows were draped with Georgian-style floor-length curtains. The original room layouts had been preserved, so even on the first floor there were only half a dozen tables—if that—giving the impression of discretion and privacy. This evening several tables were still unoccupied, and he hoped Flavia would not feel crowded or under observation. He wanted her to feel at ease.

Restlessly, he glanced around, anticipation flickering within him. He'd waited so long for this—and now, finally, it was about to start. He had checked with the driver of the car he'd sent for her—she would be here any minute…

And there she was! Pausing in the doorway. One of the restaurant staff was ushering her in, indicating his table to her with an unobtrusive murmur. For a moment she was completely still, but Leon did not mind. He was drinking her in.

Seeing her again, in the flesh and not just in his memory, was confirming everything that had drawn his eye from the first. That perfect bone structure, the clear eyes, the oval frame of her face, the long, slender throat and her beautiful, graceful figure—all was just as he remembered. Yes—she was exactly what he wanted.

His eyes worked over her assessingly, the slightest twist tugging at his mouth.

She was dressed with an even greater austerity of style than she had been that first evening at the cocktail party at her father's apartment. Not only was her hair tightly drawn back into a sleek chignon, and her make-up subtle to the point of being understated, but she was wearing a knee-length dress in dark grey, with a little stand-up collar and sleeves that reached almost to her elbows. All that brightened her was a single row of pearls, and pearl studs at her earlobes.

He got to his feet, and as if a switch had been turned on in her back she started to walk towards him. She looked very pale, but he thought that might be because of the low lighting from the wall sconces. As she took her place at their table, the candelabra to one side gave her pale flesh a warmer glow.

He sat down opposite her, letting his eyes rest on her in appreciation.

'You came,' he said.

She inclined her head, reaching for her linen napkin, which she flicked across her lap. The barest smile, the least that would pass muster in a social situation, fleeted across her mouth.

The mouth that opened to mine—that tasted of honey, and roses, and all the delights that she promised with that kiss...

His eyes flickered. Well, those delights would come now. It was impossible that they should not. Now she wanted them as much as he did. Her presence here was proof of that.

As he let her settle herself, let the waiter pour her water, proffer menus to them both and the wine list to himself, he contented himself with looking, not talking.

She was still not meeting his eyes, and for a moment there was a darkening glint in his. Then enlightenment dawned. It was obvious—the set of her shoulders, the ramrod-straightness of her back, the way she wouldn't look at him, the briefness of her smile not just to him but to the waiter as well. All showed one thing only.

She was nervous.

It was as clear as a bell. *That* was what was constraining her. Nerves. And she was nervous, Leon knew with every male instinct, because she was doing exactly what he wanted her to do—being ultra-aware of him.

Ultra-aware of the fact that *he* knew, and *she* knew, and they *both* knew that they had shared an embrace that meant she could never—not for a moment—go back to the way she had been before that embrace: pretending to him, to herself, that she was not responsive to him.

But she didn't know how to handle that—that was why she was sitting there so stiffly, so nervously. Well, she need not be nervous. This time he would not rush her, as he had so rashly before, overcome with wanting her. He would give her the time she needed to feel at ease with him.

To come with him on the journey he would take her on— deep, deep into the sensual heart of the passion that he knew with absolute certainty awaited them together.

But that was for later. Much later. For now, they were dining together. Getting to know each other. Starting their relationship.

He opened his menu and, slightly jerkily, she did likewise. He gave her time to peruse it, then made some passing observations and some suggestions. Stiltedly, she made her choice.

How she was going to manage to swallow, she didn't know. Tension was racking through her, tightening her throat, churning her stomach. She seemed to be frozen inside, and for that she was abjectedly grateful. It was though she were watching the world from inside a glacier—a glacier that was keeping her safe inside its icy depths. Numbing her with its cold.

If only, she thought desperately, it could numb her other senses! If only she didn't have to sit here looking at him, listening to him, hearing his voice—that dark, accented voice that seemed to resonate deep within her—her eyes trying to blank him out and failing utterly, totally.

The moment she'd walked into the room her eyes had gone to him instantly, as if drawn by some giant magnet. The image that had been burning on her retina since she'd flung herself out of his limo had leapt into life, imprinting itself on the flesh-and-blood man. Despite her frozen insides, she had felt her throat tighten as her body responded to him. And now, sitting so close to him, his presence was impinging on her so that she was ultra-aware of him. Of the strong, compelling features, the dark, expressive eyes, the breadth of his shoulders sheathed in the dark charcoal jacket, the sable hair that caught the light from the candelabra.

Deep within the frozen core of her body she could feel the layers of ice shift and fracture...

Hatred for what her father was making her do writhed within her. Her consciousness of the lie she was parading in front of Leon Maranz was like a snake in her mind—the lie of behaving as though she were here willingly, as if her hand had *not* been forced by her father in the most compelling way he could devise.

For a moment, as her eyes rested on the man opposite her, she felt a flaring impulse within her.

Tell him! Tell him the truth of why you are here with him tonight! Tell him what your father is threatening you with! You have no right to be here under such false pretences—no right to deceive him, pretend that you haven't been forced into this!

But she couldn't—didn't dare. Cold ran in her veins. What if she did tell Leon Maranz the truth about what her father was making her do and he was so angry that he then walked away from bailing out her father? Let her father go down the tubes.

The cold intensified. If that happened she knew with absolute certainty that her father would revenge himself on her by foreclosing on Harford. Punish her for not saving him.

So there was nothing she could do—nothing at all. She had to live out this lie. Do what her father ordered. Continue with this tormenting ordeal that was tearing her apart...

The wine had been poured and Leon was raising his glass 'To a new beginning for us.'

His voice was slightly husky, and Flavia could feel it resonate within her. Feel the pressure of his dark gaze on her. Her eyelashes dropped over her eyes, veiling them, as she took a tiny sip of her own wine.

Leon set down his glass. 'I wanted to thank you for accepting my invitation this evening,' he said, his voice low and measured.

Her fingers tightened around the stem of her glass. The lie of what she was doing—she had not accepted his invitation at all; she had been manipulated and forced into it by her father—screamed silently in her head. But there was nothing she could say—nothing.

'And I wanted to apologise to you. Apologise for the way I behaved when I was taking you home—and you felt you had to flee from me.'

There. He had said it. He'd known he'd have to—that it was the only way forward with her, to ease the strain between them. Now, though, two spots of colour flared in her cheeks, and he could see her expression blank completely. *Damn.* Maybe he shouldn't have said anything at all! Maybe that infamous English reserve meant that even his apologising was embarrassing to her!

Or maybe—the thought sliced into his mind like an acid-tipped stiletto—maybe the reason for her tension was quite different...

Like sharp stabs, words darted through his mind.

Maybe her tension is because she does not want to be here at all. What if she is here only because she now realises I am likely to bail out her father?

His expression darkened. Was that the bald, blunt truth of it? He could feel his thoughts running on unstoppably, ineluctably.

Because if that's so—if that's the only reason she's here, the only reason she's putting up with me—then...

Then *what*? That was what he had to decide. But even as he thought it he knew what the answer had to be.

Then there could be no future for them. None.

If she is not here because she wants to be—of her own volition, because she is as drawn to me as I to—then we end this right now! Whatever the strength of my desire for her, I will not succumb to it.

He could feel emotion roil within him as suspicion barbed him with poisonous darts. The ghosts of his past trailed their cold tendrils in his head. Who did she see as she sat there, the epitome of her class and her well-bred background, all pearl necklace and crystalline vowels? Did she see nobody but some jumped-up foreigner, utterly alien to her, distasteful and beneath her? Someone to look down on—look through—because, however much money he had, he could never be someone to keep company with, to be intimate with…?

Was *that* the kind of woman Flavia Lassiter was?

He watched her toy with her knife, straightening it minutely, then drop her hand to her lap to pick up her linen napkin, dabbing it momentarily to her lips, dropping it again to her lap, smoothing it out. Her gaze was fixed on it, on anything that wasn't him. Small, jerky, awkward movements, indicating glaringly how totally ill at ease she was.

Because she was embarrassed about desiring him or just embarrassed by his company?

The damnable thing was it was impossible to tell. Impossible to know what was going on inside her head. Was she essentially cut from the same cloth as her father, who had not troubled to hide his sense of superiority to those not from his privileged world? Did her outer beauty conceal an inner ugliness?

Or was there, as he so fervently hoped, more to her than that?

He *had* to find out.

Their waiter had approached, and was ready to set down their first course. Leon watched Flavia turn her head and smile at him as he carefully placed the plate in front of her, murmur thank you to him. That was a good sign, he realised. Not everyone bothered to acknowledge waiters. He felt reassurance go through him. Then it wavered again. It was easy for women like Flavia Lassiter to be gracious towards those who served them—it didn't mean they regarded them as their social equals.

He glanced at her plate as she lifted her fork to make a start.

'That looks very frugal,' he observed, referring to the scattered salad leaves and slivers of asparagus.

She gave a constrained flicker of a smile—the barest acceptable. 'I'm not very hungry,' she replied, focussing her gaze on her food, not Leon.

Leon's eyes washed over her. 'You are very slender,' he observed, meaning it as a compliment.

She didn't reply, only gave that brief, constrained flicker in response, and reached for her glass of mineral water. Her movements were still stiff and jerky. Leon cast about for another subject, as he started in on his own first course, an array of seafood.

'What do you think of the restaurant?' he enquired conversationally.

Flavia glanced around. 'It's very...good,' she said, having sought for an appropriate word, and only coming up with 'good'.

'I thought you might prefer somewhere like this to anywhere more flashy and crowded.'

The hesitant indentation of her lips in acknowledgement came again as she gathered some asparagus onto her fork. 'Oh, yes. Thank you. I do.'

Even to her own ears her voice sounded staccato and disjointed. She tried again, looking about her, knowing that she had to make an effort, that she owed him that, at least, however impossible—*totally* impossible!—her presence here was.

'I like the way it's been furnished, in eighteenth-century style,' she managed to say.

He must have sensed the unspoken approval in her voice, for she heard him say, as he took a mouthful of his wine, 'Do you like historic houses?'

Without thinking, she glanced across at him. 'Yes. I live in one.'

He frowned slightly. 'Your father's apartment is very modern, its style ultra-contemporary,' he said.

She looked at him. 'I don't live there,' she said.

Leon's expression changed. 'Your father didn't say—'

Flavia's face tightened. 'No, I doubt he did.' Her voice was clipped.

'So where *do* you live?' Leon was intrigued, realising just how little he knew about her. 'Do you have your own flat in London?'

'No.' The rejection of such an idea was audible in her voice.

'So where…?' He let the question trail.

Flavia bit her lip. The last thing she wanted to risk was Leon finding out about Harford. He might start asking questions about it she dared not answer.

'In the country,' she said shortly, keeping it deliberately vague. 'I don't like cities.'

He was looking at her curiously and she could see he was about to pursue the subject. She knew she must head him off instantly. It was dangerous ground—far, far too dangerous!

'How…how does eighteenth-century style in Britain compare with its equivalent in South America?' she asked, trying to find an anodyne topic, the kind of neutral small talk she made when at her father's social gatherings, to draw him away from her own situation. 'I've never been anywhere in Latin America, but the historic colonial style is very distinctive, and so attractive—both in the town houses and in the country *estancias*.'

Leon's voice, when he replied, was dry. 'Yes, indeed. For those few fortunate enough to live in such style. Unfortunately most of the population does not. It was not until I visited my country for the first time in a dozen years since I left for Europe that I was able to set foot in such a property—one that had been converted into a luxury hotel. Until then my only experience of accommodation in my native land was in a shanty town.'

Flavia stared. Frowned. 'A shanty town?' she echoed.

'A *favela*—though strictly speaking that is a Brazilian term.' He paused, looking at her openly astonished expression. Questioning it. 'I was raised in a city slum,' he said. 'I came to this country, penniless, at the age of fifteen.'

Flavia set down her fork. 'I had no idea,' she said.

Leon's frown deepened. Could it be true that she had no

idea of his background? There had been astonishment in her voice.

But not revulsion.

He could feel hope flare within him again. Were his doubts about her unnecessary? Let them be so…

'How did you manage to get here?' she asked. There was genuine enquiry in her voice, interlaced with her astonishment.

She wanted to know? Well, he would tell her. Tell her the grim, difficult story of his rise from penury to wealth. See how she reacted to it.

'I came with my uncle—he spent his life savings getting us here. He wanted a better future for me, his dead sister's son, than could ever have been possible at home.'

She was still staring at him. 'But how on *earth* did you manage to get from that to…to what you are now?'

There was a note of disbelief in her voice, as if she thought he must be exaggerating the poverty of his origins. But what there was *not*, Leon could tell—and the realisation surged through him—was any note of repugnance or revulsion at his lowly start in life.

'I worked,' he said simply. 'To anyone from the Third World Europe is a place of incredible opportunity to make good. So I worked non-stop. And, though it was hard, little by little I put money aside. My uncle, to my grief, became ill three years later and died, but by then I was on my way. I studied at evening college to understand the financing of business, and did any work going to increase my savings.'

He warmed to his theme, feeling memories leap in his head from a dozen years ago. 'What I spent them on was others like me, striving to make good. I chose very carefully, and if I thought they were serious and dedicated, and above all, hardworking, I loaned them the small amounts of money that they needed to buy inventory, rent premises, machinery, transport—to start their own businesses. I took a share in their profits—a fair one, no more as they prospered, and little by little I prospered, too. I increased my investments, my loans, nearly always amongst the immigrant community who understood—still understand—how much the West has in comparison with the Third World, how hard work can lift them out of poverty with an ease that is almost impossible in the Third World primarily because of the lack of credit, the mass poverty there. And that is why,' he finished, 'now that my investments are on a corporate scale, and my profits, too, I run an extensive financing programme in microloans and similar on-the-ground investment back in South America.'

There was a caustic note in his voice now, Flavia heard, listening with growing astonishment and attention as he went on. 'Some economists who are used to vast government-backed investments from the global banking community, and they might consider my efforts small fry. But—' his eyes narrowed, becoming piercing with his intense emotion '—they have never lived in those shanty towns, never realised that it is individuals who are poor—not populations. National prosperity is built from the ground up, family by family, and *that* is my focus. My goal. My mission in life.'

He fell silent at last, burningly conscious that he had done something he had never done before—bared his soul about what was most important in his work. She was gazing at him, lips parted. The expression in her eyes was different from any he had yet seen there.

And it filled him with an emotion he had never yet felt.

'I think it's extraordinary,' she said quietly. 'An extraordinary achievement.' She paused, picked up her fork again. 'No wonder you think me shallow and spoilt for not working.' Her voice was small, subdued, and she would not look at him.

Emotion was coursing through Leon. Not just because he had bared his soul, but because of how Flavia had reacted. Relief—more than relief—leapt in his breast.

She didn't know I was born poor—and she is not offended or contemptuous of it!

If there was any hint of contempt it was for herself.

He was swift to dissolve it.

'None of us is responsible for our background. Only for what we do, how we live our lives, the decisions we make,' he said.

It was meant to be a gentle remark, a soothing one. Yet before his eyes her face changed. The animation that had been there a moment ago as she'd spoken to him vanished. Tension leapt again, and it was as if a mask had shut down over her. Her eyes dropped and she swallowed, reaching for her wine glass.

She took a mouthful, feeling the need for it. His words burnt like a new brand on her skin. Consciousness of what she was doing here—why she was there, at whose bidding and for what purpose—scalded her. But there was nothing she could do—*nothing*! If she did not go along with what her father wanted he would turn her grandmother out of the house she loved, sell it from under her feet, without pity or compunction or remorse.

But if she'd felt bad before about what she was doing at her father's behest, now, having heard just what kind of man Leon Maranz truly was, she was excruciated.

I thought him just one more fat cat financier, born to some wealthy South American family, cocooned in money, caring only about the next profit-making deal to be made.

The truth was utterly different.

Involuntarily her eyes went to him again, seeing for the first time not the five-thousand-pound Savile Row suit, the silk tie, the gold watch snaking around his lean wrist—all the appurtenances of wealth and luxury. Seeing something quite different.

The young, impoverished, desperate immigrant, striving with all his determination, all his dedication and perseverance, to transform his destiny from what would have awaited him in his place of birth—the teeming, fetid *favela*—to one he had wrought for himself out of the opportunities he had been given in coming to Europe, to the rich Western world.

And not just for himself. Leon Maranz had not turned his back on his origins, not left his compatriots to rot, but had determined to use the wealth he'd made to help lift them out of the same poverty he'd once known. He'd have to have faith in them, offered them a chance just as he'd once had.

Emotions clashed within her. One, she knew, was a strong, bright glow—a shining sense of admiration for what Leon Maranz had achieved, was still achieving. An admiration that brought with it something else.

He's a man I need have no reservations about, no qualms— he's free from the venal, avaricious taint of my father, who built his fortune ruthlessly and without any compunction for anyone else. He's nothing like my father—for all his wealth— nothing like him at all!

Yet even as the realisation sent that glow through her it brought in its wake more bitter anguish. A burning, shaming consciousness of being her despised father's tool, being used by him for his own ends, forced into deceit, manipulation, lies, to safeguard what she held so dear.

It was unbearable—unbearable!

Her eyes dropped again, tension once more racking her body.

Across the table, Leon watched the transformation. He had almost broken through the web of constraint and nerves that had been so visibly possessing her since she had walked into the restaurant—almost! But now it had webbed around her again, and she was back to being as tense as a board...

For the rest of the evening he strove to break through again, to see once more that spark of contact, of communication with her. But it was gone. Extinguished. All he could achieve was a strained, awkward conversation, with him doing nearly all the talking, about one anodyne subject after another. Frustration bit in him. Just as she'd started to thaw towards him she'd frozen solid again. Yet something had changed between them, making his fears about her attitude towards him dissolve. And on that he could build—work. Work to rekindle that small but so-revealing spark of human warmth he had seen in her. Work to draw her out, draw her to him—win her to him.

And if that took time—well, so be it, then.

He accepted her halting conversation, making the evening as easy for her as he possibly could. And when the meal was over he thanked her for her company, evinced his pleasure at it, told her his car would take her back to her father's apartment and then asked if he might see her again.

Flavia stood on the pavement outside the restaurant. At the kerb the large black limo was hovering, its driver dutifully holding open the door for her. Leon was smiling down at her.

'Can I persuade you, if not to Shakespeare, then to something else at the theatre? Is there anything playing that might tempt you? Or perhaps,' he elaborated, wanting to give her not the least reason to turn down his seeing her again, 'you might prefer the opera, or a concert? Or what about an art exhibition?' he finished, wanting to give her as many options as he could in the fervent hope that something—anything!—might trigger her interest, be the key to break down her constraint.

But all he got was a low-pitched, awkward, 'I don't really mind… Whatever you would like…'

What I would like, thought Leon frustratedly, *is what* you *would like.* But all he said in response to her lukewarm reply was a measured, 'Well, I'll see what I can come up with, OK?' He delivered it with a smile he hoped was reassuring and complaisant. Then, in a slightly brisker tone, he said, 'Till tomorrow, then—will seven o'clock be all right for you?'

'Yes. Thank you. Thank you for this evening. Um—goodnight.'

She flickered her hesitant social smile at him and climbed into the car, murmuring a semi-audible thank you to the driver holding the door. Then she sank back into the deep leather of the interior.

Misery writhed within her. Seeing Leon Maranz again had been a torment of exquisite proportions! To sit opposite him, across that small table lit by candlelight, to want to do nothing more than drink in everything about him! But to be every single moment tormentingly conscious that she was there at her father's bidding, the tool of his machinations—pimped out to the man he wanted to save his riches for him...

Shame burnt along every nerve-ending, inflamed with anger at her father—anger at his threat to her frail, vulnerable grandmother; anger that he was prepared to use his own daughter to try and save his sorry skin; and anger, above all—the realisation came like a blow to the heart—that he was poisoning something that could have been so incredibly special to her.

For the first time in my life I have met someone like no one I have ever met before! Whatever it is about Leon Maranz, he can affect me as no one else ever has! For the first time, I have known what desire truly is...

But it had been poisoned by deceit. Polluted by her father's blackmail.

Making it impossible for her to be as she truly wanted to be with Leon. Making her frozen with the shame twisting inside her like wires of guilt. Holding him at bay because of the unspoken lie between them, the threat hanging over her head that she dared not tell him about yet which held her in unbreakable talons.

Misery welled dully within her as Leon's car drove her away. Back to the father she hated with all her being for what he was doing to her. Making a cruel mockery of her tormented, anguished feelings.

Alone on the pavement, Leon watched the car disappear into the London traffic. Frustration warred within him, against a steely determination. There must be a way of getting through to her! A way to persuade her to finally lower her guard against him and start to respond to him. He had seen a precious, essential glimpse of it as he'd told her of his background—but then she had clammed up again!

But at least, he reasoned, as he hailed a taxi to take him

back to his apartment, she'd agreed to see him again—and the very next night. He had till then to come up with something that might appeal to her—something that might help her relax a little towards him. But what? She'd sounded nothing more than polite about any of his suggestions.

His brow furrowed as the taxi turned into Shaftesbury Avenue. All around London buzzed and blared with noise from the traffic, garish neon lights from the shops, restaurants and the theatres that lined the road, and the pavements were thronged with people out for the evening. Suddenly it dawned on him. An echo of her terse comment when he'd asked where she lived sounded in his memory.

'I don't like cities.'

Of *course*—that was it! Enlightenment hit him. No matter how carefully he'd chosen the restaurant tonight, it was London itself she didn't care for.

Relief at his realisation filled him. He slid his mobile out of his breast pocket and tapped in an internet search. Moments later he'd connected to the phone number provided and made the reservation he wanted.

He sat back, his shoulders relaxing into the seat. Tomorrow night would be very, very different from tonight. He was sure of it.

He shut his eyes, letting the image of Flavia, in all her beauty, infuse his retinas.

CHAPTER EIGHT

'THE limo's here, sweetie. Don't keep him waiting!'

Anita's voice was sugared, but Flavia could hear an acid note in it as well. Her father's girlfriend was making a poor job of failing to conceal both her irritation and her jealousy of her. As she walked past the other woman, Flavia could see Anita, glass of wine lolling from scarlet-tipped fingers, subjecting her to a scornful scrutiny.

'God, I hope he's got a taste for seducing nuns!' Anita sneered. 'Why the hell you don't take my advice on how to dress to impress, I don't know!'

Yes, well, thought Flavia silently, making no comment, *that depends on just what impression one wants to make*. Her eyes flicked dismissively over Anita's clingy leopard-print dress.

She knew what impression *she* herself wanted to make, and the round-necked, sleeveless black shift over which she wore a silk-knit jacket fitted the bill. As she reached the front door, she caught a last jibe from Anita.

'I hope you've got a spare pair of knickers for the morning in your handbag, sweetie. We don't want to see you back here tonight! This time make sure you don't cop out—just do whatever it takes to keep Leon happy. Your father's counting on it. Or ga-ga Granny'll be popping her senile clogs in a council house. And don't think your father won't see to it! If he goes down—*you* go down!' she promised venomously. 'So keep that gorgeous Latino hunk of yours sweet on us, if you know what's good for you!' Her tone changed, becoming barbed and accusatory. 'It's not like it's going to be any kind of bloody ordeal, is it? Going to bed with a guy like that! So stop looking like Little Miss Martyr! Hell, I'd trade places with you like a shot—believe me!' She took another swig from her wine glass, and glared balefully at Flavia.

Face set, jaw as tight as steel, hatred for her father and for Anita biting in her blood, Flavia snapped the apartment door shut behind her, shutting out Anita's crude, cruel words, her sleazy innuendo, and stalking towards the lift. Mortification burned in her—and shame, and anger, and bitter, bitter resentment. All twisting and writhing like snakes.

But as she walked out of the apartment block she crushed her tormenting emotions back down inside her. The evening stretched ahead of her, and there was nothing she could do about it.

Leon's driver was getting out of the car, tipping his cap to her as he opened the rear passenger door, and she stepped inside. But as she sank back into the seat she froze.

Leon was also in the car.

For a moment she felt panic flare in her eyes. She subdued it as swiftly as she could, stiffly returning his greeting as the car pulled away.

Leon gave her time to compose herself whilst, with a catch in his throat, he took in just how stunningly beautiful she looked all over again. The black of the dress, severe though it was, illuminated the pearlescence of her skin, the soft sheen of her hair in its customary chignon. And the faint floral scent she was wearing was winding into his senses. How incredibly beautiful she was! Emotion welled through him, and for a moment he could only drink her in.

But he could see that she was just as tense tonight—there was no lowering of her guard. Determination scythed through him. Well, perhaps this evening would be more propitious...

'You said last night,' he began, 'that you would be happy to let me choose what to do this evening. So...' He took a breath.

'I hope I've made a good choice. Tell me—' he looked at her enquiringly '—have you ever been to Mereden?'

She looked slightly confused. 'Mereden? No. I've heard of it, but...' She paused. 'Isn't it way out of London?'

He nodded. 'Yes. You let slip last night that you didn't care for cities, so I thought you might enjoy somewhere like Mereden instead. It shouldn't take more than maybe half an hour to get there. I hope that's OK with you?'

'Um—yes. Yes. Of course.'

He threw a glancing smile at her. 'Good. While we're travelling there, I hope you won't mind if I use the time to finish off some work. There's some magazines if you'd like something to flick through.'

Relieved that she did not have to make painful conversation with him yet, Flavia took one of the magazines at random while Leon focussed on his laptop. Every sense was super-aware of him sitting there, a few feet away from her, and every part of her mind was leaping with the memory of what had happened the last time she'd sat in this limo with him...

He'd swept away her reserve, her resistance, as if they were nothing. Nothing at all! Melting her with his kiss, dissolving her very bones with it!

It had been the most devastating experience of her life—changing everything she'd been. Making her feel what she had never felt before!

She could feel her heart-rate quicken as the memory seared across her brain, feel her breath catch. Urgently she fought for control, lest he turn his head, see the hectic flush in her cheeks—and know just what had caused it.

Somehow she managed to regain at least an outer semblance of the composure she was trying to hang on to with all her might. Inwardly, her emotions were in turmoil—currents swirling inchoately as she tried not to think about what might lie ahead at the end of the evening...

She was grateful for the journey out of London. By the time the car was making its way off the motorway into the

Thames Valley she was able to take some cognisance of where
they were going. They were driving through hilly woodland
along quiet, country roads that seemed a universe away from
London, only that short journey behind them.

The car slowed to turn through imposing ironwork gates,
to move along a drive bordered by rhododendrons in vivid
bloom, with glimpses of extensive parkland beyond. Early
evening sunshine lit up the landscape, and Flavia could not
help but feel its soothing influence over her jangled nerves.

'Better than London?'

Leon's enquiry made her turn her head. He had shut down
his laptop and was slipping it into its case.

'Oh, yes…'

There was a warmth in her voice that was obvious by its
previous absence. As the magnificent Palladian frontage of
Mereden came into view, bathed in sunlight and lapped by
manicured gardens, he knew with satisfaction that he had
made a good decision in bringing Flavia here. She was no
city girl, craving bright lights and crowds. This country house
hotel, set in rural parkland, was far more her style!

They drew up in front of the grand entrance and a uni-
formed doorman stepped forward to open the passenger door.
Flavia climbed out and looked around her. She had heard
of Mereden, but had never been here before. Once a stately
home, now it was a lavish private hotel, set in the exclusive
wealthy catchment area of the Thames Valley.

'Shall we go in?'

Leon ushered her forward and she stepped through the
imposing double doorway into a high-ceilinged hall beyond.

They were clearly expected, and were conducted out on to
a wide terrace overlooking the gardens and the River Thames
beyond. Guests were enjoying pre-dinner drinks, watching
the sunset. Flavia caught her breath, gazing out over the pan-
oramic vista.

'Worth the drive out?'

She turned impulsively to Leon. 'Oh, yes! It's absolutely breathtaking!'

His expression stilled. Slowly he replied, 'I'm glad you like it.'

'Who couldn't?' she answered, and turned back to gaze over the stone balustrade at the verdant lawns, drenched in golden evening sunlight, reaching down towards the river's edge.

Even without consciously realising it, she could feel some of the tension racking through her ebb a little. It was *so* good to be out of London, away from the built-up streets, in such a glorious place as this, with such a vista in front of her. It was impossible not to respond to it. The warm, balmy air, clean and fresh after the fumes and pollution of London, was like a blessing, as was the blessed quietness all around her. No traffic noise was audible, only the murmuring of the other guests, and the evening birdsong from the trees set around the wide lawns.

'Madam?' A waiter was standing beside her, champagne glasses on a tray.

'Thank you,' she found herself saying with a smile, and took a narrow flute filled with gently fizzing liquid.

Leon did likewise. A sense of achievement glowed in him. He'd definitely done the right thing in bringing her here. He could feel relief easing through him, and hoped it was not premature. But, for all his wariness, at least her reaction so far was proving encouraging.

'To a pleasant evening,' he said.

With only the barest hesitation Flavia clinked her flute to his, then, as if to give herself some cover, turned back to gaze out over the vista, sipping at the champagne. It tasted cold and delicious.

'I don't know how anyone can live in London,' she heard herself musing, her eyes resting on the peaceful scenery before her.

Leon moved slightly and came to stand beside her, taking care not to invade her body space lest she take fright. He rested a hand on the sun-warmed stone of the balustrade.

'Many don't have another choice,' he pointed out mildly. What he didn't point out, though, was that her comment was the first completely unprompted one she'd made to him. He wanted to do absolutely nothing to make her aware of that. If that meant treading on eggshells, so be it.

Her eyes flickered to him, then swiftly away out over the view again. 'Yes. I feel so sorry for them. But some people like the city. My father and Anita, for example.' Her voice was flat.

'I hated London when I first came,' Leon said, choosing not to take up her remark about her father and his girlfriend. 'It was freezing cold, and it rained all the time.'

'A lot of foreigners think that,' she said wryly. 'Quite a few Brits, too—it's why they head south to the sun. But somehow winter is worse in the city, I think.'

'I wouldn't disagree with you there,' said Leon dryly. He paused. 'So, whereabouts in the country do you live?'

Immediately he saw her stiffen. Inwardly he cursed himself. Up till now, ever since they'd arrived here, she'd seemed to thaw discernibly—as if the beautiful, rural surroundings had calmed her. Now the tension was back in the set of her shoulders.

'Oh, in the West Country,' she said, offhandedly. 'Look, isn't that a heron?'

Her voice was animated because she wanted to change the subject fast. It was the second time Leon had asked her where she lived, and it was the last thing she wanted him to know. Disquiet swirled rancidly within her at the reminder of just why she was here—and at whose bidding. For a brief moment there seemed to be a shadow over the sunlit view she was gazing over.

Thankfully, he accepted her change of tack. 'I wouldn't know,' he said. 'Natural history isn't my thing at all.'

'I think it *is* a heron,' she said, eyes fixed on it.

'What are those smaller birds darting around over the river?' If she wanted to talk about wildlife, then he could only be grateful. Anything to keep her mood as it was. The stiffening in her shoulders as he'd asked about where she lived had gone again, and he was thankful. He didn't want to talk about anything at all that might make her tense up again. This visible thawing, slight though it was, was far too precious for that.

'Swallows and swifts, probably,' she replied. 'They like to catch the insects that are attracted to the water.' She took another sip from her champagne flute. It helped to let her speak more naturally, with less awkward stiffness. And besides, sipping chilled champagne, here on the terrace, looking out over so beautiful a vista, seemed an appropriate thing to do in such a setting.

With such a man beside her... A man who set every nerve-ending in her body aflame...

No—she mustn't think of that! Mustn't let herself. She was coping with this whole situation in the only way she could—by taking it minute by minute and keeping that composed, unemotional mask over her face, her mind...

Leon smiled. 'Ah, yes—I've seen them at my villa on Santera, skimming over the swimming pool in the evenings.'

Flavia glanced at him. 'Santera?'

'One of the many smaller islands of the Balearics,' he said.

'I've not heard of it.' She shook her head slightly.

'Most people haven't,' he answered. 'They know about the main islands of the Balearics—notably Majorca—but the archipelago has a host of other tiny islands and islets. Many are uninhabited, kept as nature reserves or just places to sail to and around. A few have villas and resorts on them, like Santera.'

Flavia looked away again. It was safer to look at the view down to the river, to study the birds darting over the water, than to stand looking at Leon. He was talking again, and she was grateful. More about this island near Majorca. She made herself pay attention. Nature, geography, foreign travel—all were safe, innocuous subjects.

'Santera is very flat,' he was saying, 'and the land almost seems to meld with the sea. It's dry and sandy, but to my mind very lovely. The beaches are wonderful, and there is only one metalled road, leading from the small harbour where supplies are brought in. There are only a few other villas there besides mine, so each is very secluded.'

'It sounds beautiful,' she said slowly. There had been a warmth in his voice she had not heard before, and it made her turn her head to glance at him. Just for a moment—the briefest second—their gazes mingled.

Then she pulled hers away and looked out towards the River Thames again, rotating the stem of her champagne glass. Her blood seemed to be swirling in her veins suddenly.

'It is,' he said. An idea was forming in his mind, though he was not sure of it yet. 'But it is not by any means luxurious.'

She gave a small, dismissive shrug of her shoulders. 'Luxury isn't important,' she said.

His eyes narrowed, studying her as she gazed out over the balustrade. She was a child of luxury—born to it—with a wealthy father to lavish her with designer clothes like the elegant outfit she was wearing now.

'Easy to say when you have always had it at your disposal,' he could not stop himself saying.

She turned at that. Her expression was stricken, and Leon immediately felt bad that he'd made such a remark.

'I'm sorry,' she said, 'that was crass of me.' There was a sincerity in her voice that was not there just for politeness.

He would have responded, but one of the hotel staff was approaching, enquiring if they would care to take their table yet.

Their table was by the French windows and gave a full view of the setting sun, its rays gilding the ornate room and glinting on the polished silverware. Menus were presented, their flutes refilled, and whether it was the champagne or the air of the countryside, Flavia suddenly felt hungry. When she gave her order, Leon looked mildly surprised at her choices. They were definitely more hearty than they had been the night before.

'It all sounds so appetising,' she said by way of explanation.

When the food arrived, superbly presented and even more superbly prepared, she found she was eating with real enjoyment.

Something was changing, she knew. It wasn't just the champagne, or even the exquisite food, or the beautiful room they were dining in—all painted Adam ceiling and gilded pillars, opening out on to the terrace and the view beyond. It was more than that.

Her gaze went to Leon.

For a long, long moment her eyes rested on him, taking him in, drinking him in. She felt an aching longing welling inside her. And knew she must answer a question she could no longer avoid, no longer hide from.

If I were free—totally free, without any consideration for anyone but myself—where would I be?

She had fled from Leon once, overwhelmed by him, by the feelings he could arouse in her, seeing only the impossibility of it all, scared and overcome by it. She had fled back home to her responsibilities, to the grandmother who depended on her. Leon Maranz was not for her—he could not be. The inescapable circumstances of her life made it impossible.

But now she had been forced to go to him. Forced to do her father's foul bidding. She resented and hated it. Yet for all that the question came again, refusing to be silenced.

If I were totally free—if I could choose for myself—where would I be?

And the answer came clear, with no possibility of denial.

I would be here. Here with Leon.

Because there has never been anyone like him before in my life and being with him is all I want!

It was a truth she could no longer deny. Yet even as she accepted it she felt the cry come from deep within her.

If only... If only I were here with him without anything to do with my father! Without the hideous pressure he is putting on me! If only I were here with Leon and the threat to Harford, to my grandmother, never existed! If only my father had not tainted and befouled what I want so much! This time with Leon...this precious time!

Because if that were so... If that were so, she knew, with deep, absolute certainty, that she would be here willingly, joyously. With absolute conviction in what she was doing. Giving in to the overpowering need to succumb to what he had lit within her like a flame.

There has never been anyone like him—never been anything like the response he evokes in me! Never before—and never again...

Why it had happened she could not tell. Why this man she did not know. She knew only that it was so—that it had happened—and she could no more deny it or defy it than cease to breathe. The truth of it was as radiant as the sun setting in liquid fire, its last rays streaming all around her, turning the world to gold.

Anguish clutched at her. That what she felt for Leon, this extraordinary flame of burning desire, should be so sullied by what her father was doing to her was unbearable—unbearable that her father should be soiling it with his foul demands and threats! Making something shameful of what should have been so wonderful!

And then, as she gazed at him, her anguish in her face, his eyes met hers. Blazed with sudden desire impossible to veil. And in that moment, as she met the full charge, she felt something shift and change and resolve in her.

So what if her father was trying to exploit her for his own ends? Trying to manipulate her, threatening and blackmailing her, making her feel soiled and ashamed? She was doing what he wanted for her grandmother's sake—and the knowledge seared within her that it was what *she* wanted, too! What she wanted with all her being.

Words formed in her head. Strong—resolute. From the inner core of her.

What is happening is happening. I will not let what my father is doing poison and destroy it. I will not let it taint and sully it.

She would put everything aside but her own feelings for Leon. Nothing her father could do could poison *them*! She would not allow it—would not permit it! She would put aside everything her father had said, and threatened, and insinuated, and manipulated. Because one shining truth was blazing within her, as golden and glorious as the setting sun bathing the world in beauty: she was here, now, because she *wanted* to be, because she would of her own free choice be nowhere else but here, with Leon. Going forward with him to wherever he would take her, on a journey she had never taken before—on a journey into the heart of desire and its burning, incandescent fulfilment.

She would give herself to him and let nothing taint this time—*nothing*!

Like light and warmth, the resolution streamed through her, blazed from her eyes. Her gaze hung on Leon's, and in his dark, beautiful eyes she saw suddenly, like a fire kindling, an answering blaze. For one endless moment it was there—a moment of intensity she had never known before. Then, as if it was overwhelming her, like breathing pure oxygen or gazing into the heart of the too-bright sun, she dropped her gaze, breathless with sudden, extraordinary happiness.

Across the table Leon felt his senses reeling. Triumph—more than triumph!—coursed through him. For the first time he had seen in Flavia what he had so long ached to see: the fire of her response to him acknowledged, admitted—accepted. Relief filled him, deep and profound. The knowledge that finally he had broken through that endless guard she'd held up to him, keeping him at bay, holding him off. Gratitude welled within him, and resolve—resolve that her new-found trust in him would never be betrayed. He would take her only where she herself wanted to go, on the journey that awaited them into the heart of desire—desire fulfilled...

Emotion moved within him, making him pause. A sense of wonder filled him—a sense of gratitude that this beautiful, beautiful woman, as wary as a doe, had been granted to him.

I will not hurt her or let her down. I will be worthy of her. I will not betray her trust in me, so valued because it was so hard-won...

But he must still proceed slowly, carefully, he knew. She must not be rushed or overwhelmed lest she take fright again, hide once more behind that frigid wall surrounding her. He cast about for something easy to talk about—some unpressured, uncontentious topic that would help to draw her out, set her yet more at her ease, build on the fragile trust that had put forth its precious green shoots this evening.

Ironically, he knew that what he wanted was to find out much more about her. There was so little he knew—even where she lived. Well, it was no matter. Gradually, as they got to know each other fully, they would talk more about themselves, have no secrets from each other. Already, the previous evening, he had found himself telling her about his work to help others living as he once had himself—a subject he did not usually dwell on in company. There were those in the world he moved in now who found the thought of such dire poverty uncomfortable, unsettling.

Flavia hadn't seemed to, though—and it had been the sincerity of her sympathy, briefly expressed as it had been, that had shown him she was not the shallow, venal, pampered princess he'd feared she might be, given her wealthy background and given, he thought, with an inward frown, her father's utter lack of sensibility about the plight of others in the world! But Flavia was clearly cut from a different cloth from her father—he trusted that instinctively.

As if catching his thoughts, she spoke, pre-empting his mental search for a safe, neutral topic to converse on with her.

'You mentioned last night you'd set up projects to help those trapped in poverty in the Third World?' she ventured. 'What sort of enterprises are most effective?'

There was genuine interest in her enquiry. Even so, she was conscious that she was seeking a subject that would give him the role of talking the most. Her own thoughts and emotions were in freefall, and she needed time—precious time—to let them settle. Letting him talk would give her that time—time to come to terms with the momentous resolution she had made.

Time, too, to do what she so wanted to do—just sit there and drink him in. Drink in the strong, magnetic features, sit quietly and watch the lean perfection of his body, look at the dark feathered sable of his hair, the quick indentation of his lips, hear the deep accented tones of his voice. All a sensuous, breath-catching delight to her!

A sense of release filled her. As if a hideous burden had been lifted from her, freeing her from the corruptive taint of her father's venal machinations.

Now, finally, she could accept that, whatever the cause of her being here with Leon, *this* was where she wanted to be. And accept freely that it was what *she* wanted, too—to have this time with Leon, come what may.

As he started to answer her she sat, listening to him as they dined. He elaborated on the work he was doing—giving back the fruits of his own hard, long endeavours to drag himself out of the same poverty—and she set her senses free, her passions free. She would give herself joyously, willingly to Leon, to his desire for her—her desire for him.

And she would let nothing taint it, poison it.

She would not allow it.

On wings of liberation she felt her spirits soar, and happiness, relief, anticipation and joy filled her being.

CHAPTER NINE

'SHALL I extinguish the candle? You would see the stars more clearly then.'

Flavia shook her head. 'No, I think the garden lights will still make it impossible to see them well.'

They were taking coffee at the far end of the terrace, where it opened into a stone-paved parterre edged with box into which were inset small footlights. Other guests were dotted around at low tables, seated in wickerwork chairs, taking coffee and liqueurs.

'The best stars I've seen,' Leon was musing, 'are on Santera. Like gold discs cut out of black velvet. One day I'll buy a telescope—though I'll need to hire an astronomer as well, to show me what I'm looking at,' he added ruefully.

She smiled. 'I'm sure it would be a popular job,' she said.

She let her shoulders relax back into the chair, lifting her cup of coffee. Despite the liberating ease with which she now found she could converse with Leon, at the same time she could feel a sensation like a trickle of electricity rippling through her, just below the level of her skin. It was setting her heartbeat just a little more rapid, and her pulse was a little more tangible, her breath a little more uneven.

Her eyes went to the man sitting back in the wicker chair opposite her, and it seemed to her that the trickle of electricity flickering beneath her skin gave a little surge of voltage. Her gaze hung on his face—so darkly planed, so compelling to look at. His whole strong, dominating physical presence was waiting for her.

Waiting for her to be ready.

And I am—finally. That is what has happened. I am no longer fighting what I first recognised in that very first moment of seeing him. At last—despite everything my father has done, despite all my fears for my poor grandmother—this is something that I want...with all my being.

The shadow of her father, his malign presence in her life, his threatening power to destroy the last months of her grandmother's life, still hung there like a lowering cloud, but she set it aside. She would not let it poison this time that had come upon her, which finally she would accept.

Willingly, joyously, desiringly...

Her eyes met Leon's.

He knows—he knows I am ready now.

She thought he might smile, might look with satisfaction upon her, seeing her acquiescence, her acceptance, in every line of her body, the melting of her eyes. But he did not smile, and she was glad. Touched.

This was no triumph, no conquest, no victory over her doubts and resistance.

This was a mutual desiring—a shared acknowledgement of something flaring between them that both of them welcomed. Embraced.

He got to his feet. Held out a hand to her. She took it silently and let him draw her to her feet.

They walked hand in hand, and it seemed right, and real, and welcome. Strolling beside him, no words were necessary as she walked down to the far end of the terrace, where it was quiet, unpopulated by guests, unlit by floor lamps. Only the stars above glinted and gleamed in their crystal orbs.

He paused and turned, took her other hand. Gazed down into her eyes in the dim, diffused starlight.

'My Flavia,' he said.

And that was all. All she heard—all she wanted to hear.

Needed to hear. She lifted her face, let herself gaze at him, let the warmth of his hands holding hers be all the reassurance she needed.

Why this man?

She did not know. It did not matter. This moment now was all. The reasons she was here were unnecessary. Irrelevant.

'Leon…' Her voice was a breath, an exhalation, a sigh. Accepting everything he offered her. Offering him everything he craved.

He took her mouth as a flower, as the sweetest fruit. The most delicate flavour. The gentlest touch.

He was holding himself in absolute control. He knew it. Knew that this moment was precious, that it was of absolute importance that he not get it wrong this time. That this was the moment that could win him Flavia—or lose her for ever.

There would be no second chance. Not if he screwed it up now. Not if he rushed her too fast, allowed his needs to overwhelm hers.

Besides, he wanted this exquisite moment to last—to stand here beneath the stars and have her warm and pliant in his arms, as tender as the summer's night that webbed about them. Just her and him—as if alone in all the world together.

Gently, delicately, tenderly, he explored the beauty of her mouth with his, has hands cradling her head, fingertips whispering through her hair. She was leaning into him, and he felt the soft wand of her body against his, felt himself responding.

He drew away a little, released her mouth, still cradling her upturned face. There was a dazed look in her eyes, and he found himself lowering his lips to graze each fluttering eyelid.

Then, with a breath, he let his fingers slip from her completely, standing away from her.

There was a puzzled look in her starlit eyes.

'I got it wrong with you once before,' he said, his voice low, his eyes searching hers. 'I made assumptions—rushed you. This time—' he took another scissoring breath '—I won't do that. This time…' He paused, making sure he got it right this time. 'I don't want you running from me.' He paused again. 'So I ask you now: if you would like to go back to London, back to your father's apartment, I will escort you there and no further. But if you would like to stay here, at this hotel, in a room of your own, then that is what will happen. It will be exactly and only as you wish, Flavia.'

It had cost him to say what he had—but he knew he'd had to say it. Had to give her the space, the time she needed. For himself, all he ached to do was take her back in his arms, take her to a room, a bed, and finally possess her.

But this night had to be *her* choice, her choice alone, uninfluenced by him or anything else. Her free, untrammelled choice.

He let his eyes rest on her as she stood, swaying very slightly, as if being released from his hold on her had left her unsupported. He stood still—stock still. It was for her to make the next move—only her, not him. Even though it was taking every last ounce of self-control her possessed.

The expression in her eyes changed. She lifted her hand. Let her fingers graze the edge of his jaw. He had shaved before he had met her, early in the evening, but now, at this midnight hour, he could feel her fingertips encountering the slight roughness of regrowth. Her touch was electric, and he could feel every muscle in his body tense.

She gazed up at him.

'I don't know why this is,' she said, and her voice was still soft, still murmuring, but with a plaintive note in it, as though bemusement was infusing it. 'I don't know why—I only know that it is so. I only know…' Now her fingertips were tracing, with the lightest touch, the line of his lips, and his jaw tensed with the effort not to do what every sensual instinct was pounding at him to do—to catch her with his mouth, fold her into him, his hands spanning her narrow waste, and with his lips lave the slowly questing tip of her slender finger.

'I only know that I don't want to leave. I want to stay here with you.'

His hand snaked to her wrist, drawing her hand slightly away from his face. 'Are you sure—are you truly sure?' There was an intensity in his voice, in his expression, that he could not mask. Would not mask. He would hide nothing from her—as she was hiding nothing from him. He was seeing the truth of her now. He knew absolutely. This was the woman he wanted—and she wanted him. No more masks, no more ice maiden, no more chilling reserve or holding him at bay with every word she spoke. This was the woman he wanted—here, now...

'Yes...' Her voice was a breath, an exhalation.

A promise.

He lowered his head to hers, kissing her mouth lightly, sweetly. Then he tucked her hand into his, never relinquishing it for a moment, and drew her against his side.

'You'll stay with me tonight?' Leon's voice was husked. He needed to be sure—absolutely sure.

Her answer was to lean into him, brushing her cheek against his shoulder. 'Do you think,' she mused, starlight glinting in the eyes uplifted to his, 'a place like this might run to a four-poster bed?'

His mouth tugged in a smile that made Flavia's already strong beating heart catch. He dropped a lingering kiss on her mouth.

'Let's go and find out,' he said.

Hand in hand, they headed indoors.

The hotel did, indeed, have a double room with a four-poster bed. A huge one, draped in blue damask.

'It's beautiful!' Flavia exclaimed, gazing around, taking in the panelled walls, the ornamental plastered ceiling, the thick carpets and the antique furniture, all dominated by the richly hung four-poster.

'And so are you.'

The timbre of Leon's voice sent a thrumming of electricity through her and she turned to face him. Emotion swelled through her. In the low-lit room his face was strongly featured, and she could see, blazing like a dark light in his eyes, the message of his desire for her.

'Leon—'

She breathed his name, came towards him, came into his arms.

They kissed, their mouths entwining, their arms around each other, and longing quickened within her, making her breathless and amazed. When he drew away from her she felt a loss, a parting she did not want, and reached for him again.

But he smiled down at her, a slanting smile rich with promise, his eyes devouring her. 'My beautiful Flavia.'

He said her name low and resonant, and she could only gaze at him, her pulse strong and insistent in her veins.

His eyes held hers and slowly, carefully, he reached his arms around her slender back, slipping off the loose, soft jacket, feeling for the zip at the top of her dress, sliding it slowly, oh-so-slowly, down her trembling body.

As the almost bare lines of her figure were revealed by the lowering dress, his breath caught.

She was so beautiful! So slender and so poised and so perfect...

The dark shift pooled at her feet and she stepped out of it. Then, of her own volition, she raised her hands to her spine and slipped the clasp of her bra, letting it fall. She heard the rasp in Leon's voice and rejoiced in it, sliding her panties to the floor as well. It was right, it was good, it was perfect. It was what she wanted to do and it was a joyous, blessed offering to him. For a moment she just stood there, letting him feast upon her. Then, with a little smile, she lifted her hands once more to the nape of her neck and loosened her hair from its chignon.

It fell in a sensual cloud around her shoulders, and this time

Leon was no longer motionless. He caught it with his fists and lowered his head to her, drawing her naked body against his.

His mouth seared hers like a living flame, and her body was a flame in his arms. Desire surged through him, arousing, quickening his flesh. His clothes were an impediment, and with a groan he held her momentarily away from him whilst he divested himself of them. His hands were like wood, his movements clumsy in his haste and urgency, but he didn't care. He only knew that this was not a time for posed sophistication, for studied seduction. This was about the naked, blazing desire between them, the clean flame burning with the purest fuel.

As he flung his clothes aside on the nearest armchair he clasped her to him again. She gasped, knowing the strength of his desire for her. Her eyes widened in recognition. In shared arousal.

He swept her up into his arms and carried her to the waiting bed, yanking back the coverlet to lay her tenderly upon the pristine sheet. For one endless moment he simply stood and gazed down on her—on her beauteous body, bared and waiting for him, on her lustrous hair spread like a flag across the pillows, on her face, on her eyes gazing up at him with everything in that gaze that he could want.

Her desire for him—her perfect, perfect desire...

He said her name again, emotion working in his face. She lifted her arms to him, welcoming him to her, and he came down on her with all the ardour in the world, clasping her to him.

In the soft light from the low-lit bedside lamp, in the wide expanse of the bed, beneath the silken awning above them, he kissed her. He kissed her mouth and her fluttering eyes, the line of her jaw, the arch of her throat, the hollow at its base. He kissed with softly trailing lips, tender and arousing, possessing the valley between her breasts. He kissed and laved and teased and worshipped the soft ripening mounds and then their cresting coral peaks, questing ever further, down over the silken expanse of her abdomen, his hands shaping the sculpture of her hips to graze with tantalising arousal the line of the dark vee below.

He heard her gasp and felt her hands clutching at his shoulders. He lifted his head and saw hers lifting, too. He slid his strong, empowered body upwards over hers again, so that his thighs pressed down on hers, slid one limb between hers, parting her for him. His mouth sought hers, his hand cupping the nape of her neck, lifting and shaping her head to him.

His arousal was absolute, but her needs must come first. He moved to slip one hand down her breast, her flank, down to the parting of her thighs. But she caught his hand with hers.

'No—'

She gazed up at him, urgency in her eyes, and with a blaze of understanding Leon knew that she was as ready as he—that she wanted exactly what he wanted now.

'You're sure?'

His question hung only for a moment, and it was her eyes, her questing mouth seeking his afresh, that told him the answer.

And her fevered breath.

And his.

He plunged into her, deep and lifting, and she arched to meet him, her spine bowing upwards, thighs quivering beneath his as she took him into her. She cried out and he clasped her to him, his hands around her spine, supporting her. It was glorious—glorious and perfect and wondrously fulfilling as their bodies merged and fused.

He moved within her. He had to move. Could do nothing else. He was overpowered by the burning of his desire, the intensity of his arousal. And as he moved, her face was transfigured.

'Flavia!'

He saw the ecstasy take her, felt it in her body, felt it around him, pulsing like a beacon, convulsing her body. He clung to her, arms wrapped around her, held her against him as surge after surge swept through her, and he could feel the shaking of her body clasped so tight against his.

And then he could feel his own moment come.

Like a tidal wave, sweeping through his body, powerful and unstoppable. Like nothing he had ever felt before. Nothing like this!

He called out her name, his head thrown back, and gave himself to the power and the glory of the moment, feeling her body give one last, encompassing convulsion around him, taking him further than he had ever known, to lands and realms beyond, where only he and she existed...

Slowly, so slowly, their bodies eased, folding upon each other, lowering down upon the cool surface of the bed. Exhaustion came upon him, and a wake of emotion that swirled and eddied through him. He cradled her to him and she clung to him. He soothed her dampened hair, murmuring to her he knew not what, and she was boneless in his arms, her body still containing his, their limbs tumbled and entwined.

He felt the chill of the air around them now, and reaching for the coverlet drew it over them, still clutching her to him as if he would never let her go. Sleep was heavy upon him, exhaustion stilling him. He held her to him and, clasped in her arms, gave himself to sleep.

His last sliver of awareness was of her hands gentling him, her mouth tender at his lips, her voice murmuring his name.

It was all he wanted to hear in all the world.

Her voice murmuring his name...

CHAPTER TEN

'WELL, what do you think?' Leon's voice was slightly hesitant. 'I did warn you it wasn't luxurious.'

Flavia gazed about her. The single-storey villa, built in a traditional Spanish style, with whitewashed walls and red roof tiles, was framed by pine trees and gave straight on to the beach.

'It's beautiful,' she said.

Her eyes moved about, taking in the whole scene, as Leon lifted out the couple of suitcases from the Jeep he'd driven from the little quay on the far side of the island. Flavia walked forward. The low-lying ground was turfed and sandy, and she could see some goats a little way away, grazing near some bushes. There was the scent of sea in the air, and aromatic plants. And it was very hot—but the heat went with the land, and with the pale beach lapped with turquoise wavelets.

'Fancy a swim?' Leon grinned, seeing her longing glance towards the azure sea.

He carried the suitcases inside, and she followed him. The stone walls of the villa cooled the air, and the wood-shuttered windows made the atmosphere dim and shaded. Leon might have described the villa as 'not luxurious' but it was still beautifully decorated, in a rustic style with a simplicity about it that was immediately appealing to Flavia as she looked about in delight.

But then her whole world was a delight. A wonderful, entrancing delight that she had never before experienced. Her eyes rested on Leon, softening as she followed him along a tiled corridor into a large, cool bedroom and he deposited their suitcases on the wide bed. She felt her breath catch, as it did so often in these unforgettable days and nights since she had given herself to Leon.

They had spent all of the following day at Mereden. Leon had ruthlessly cancelled his business meetings to devote himself to her. They had stayed in bed till late in the morning, glorying in their unity of desire, then passed the rest of the morning exploring the beautiful grounds of the hotel, taking in a waterside lunch at the little Thameside marina the hotel provided for guests, followed by a leisurely, meandering cruise along the river in the hotel launch. They had moored under sweeping willow branches, and Leon had kissed her long and lingeringly.

'Come away with me!' he'd whispered to her. 'Come to Santera with me. Be with me completely there. We can have at least a week there—maybe two.'

Flavia's eyes had shone—then dimmed. Could she really leave her grandmother for a week or longer? Yet even while guilt had plucked at her she'd also known, with a heaviness she had long had to accept, that her grandmother would not really know how long she was away, that she would be in good hands with Mrs Stephens. And who knew? A burning longing had swept through her. Who knew how long Leon would want her? Who knew what the future might or might not hold? She could not tell and did not want to ask—wanted only to shut out everything except this bliss that was enveloping her. This joy and wonder.

A more practical objection had threaded into her mind, and as Leon had looked at her questioningly she'd said, 'I haven't got my passport.'

It didn't faze him. 'I'll send a courier for it. It can be delivered to the airport directly, and we can fly straight off tomorrow morning.'

Flavia's eyes widened. Could it really be that simple?

It was. A single phone call from the hotel's front desk had done it. Flavia had spoken directly to the courier company, giving details of where to find her passport at Harford, while Leon had contacted his PA to clear his diary and arrange flights the next day. All Flavia had then had to do was phone Mrs Stephens and arrange for her to stay longer.

'A holiday is just what you need,' her grandmother's carer had said approvingly. 'I'm happy to stay on as long as need be. Your grandmother is as well as she can be, and there is no need at all to worry.'

Relief had filled Flavia, even if there had still been an undercurrent of anxiety, a fear that she was being selfish in heading off with Leon. But as he'd swept her into his arms, and she'd found all over again the magical bliss of being together with him, her anxious thoughts about her grandmother had been swept away as well. For now—for a little while—she would be with Leon, wherever he wanted her to be.

They had paused briefly in Palma on their way to Santera, to have lunch and give Flavia an hour or two to shop for beach clothes, but now their journey was ended—and an idyll awaited them, she knew. The past and the future were held at bay—she would not think of them, would let only this sunlit present surround her, give herself entirely to the moment.

Entirely to Leon.

And she would let nothing of her fears about her grandmother, her revulsion at her father, get in the way of that.

Leon was opening her suitcase, pulling out the bikinis she'd bought in Palma that day, holding them both up.

'I can't decide which one you'll look more gorgeous in,' he told her.

She whisked them both out of his hands. 'I'll surprise you.' She laughed, and disappeared into the *en suite* bathroom she could see opening up from the bedroom.

'You have already,' murmured Leon, watching her go. His eyes were warm, his expression bemused.

But then, bemusement was a key emotion in him now—bemusement that this warmly passionate woman, whose embrace melted him, could ever have been that stiff, reserved ice maiden, holding him at bay, freezing him out. That Flavia had gone—vanished completely. This Flavia was—a revelation!

And when she reappeared a few minutes later in one of the bikinis she was a revelation again. He'd knew—intimately—just how perfect her figure was, but now, skimmed by the brief material of the swimsuit, her body was breathtaking.

Enticing.

Hurriedly he snatched up his swimming trunks and headed into the bathroom himself, adjuring Flavia to make lavish use of the sunblock they'd bought in Palma.

Within minutes they were outdoors again. 'Race you to the sea!' Flavia cried, and hared across the beach with Leon chasing after her, and both of them collapsed into the shallow turquoise waters.

Flavia lolled in the tiny wavelets, letting her head fall back, hair streaming in the water, face lifted to the sun. 'This is bliss,' she murmured, splashing idly with her feet.

It was a phrase she was to repeat over and over again. It applied, she decided, to every aspect of their days—and their nights. It was bliss to wade into the warm sea, to lounge on the shaded patio on a padded sunbed, sipping iced fruit juice at lunchtime and champagne at sunset. Bliss to have late, leisurely breakfasts, and slow, leisurely lunches, and dine on nightly barbecues beneath the starry sky which was, as Leon had promised, every bit as spectacular as he had described.

But bliss, most of all, to leave the stars to heaven and find their own in each other's arms.

They were in their own private world, Flavia knew. A world where the rest of the world did not exist. Her father's vile machinations were vanished as if they had never been. She would not think of them—or him.

Nor would she think of the reason she had succumbed to his threats.

Though her eyes shadowed, she knew she was deliberately not thinking about her grandmother. All she did was check her phone nightly for the reassuring text Mrs Stephens faithfully sent. But apart from that she let the whole world of Harford slip away. Focussing only on Leon. Only on her time with him.

How can it be so good? How can he overwhelm me the way he does? Sweeping me away, time after time, after time, into such bliss?

But it was more than passion, she knew, searingly intense as that was. It was a sense of ease with him. A togetherness. A naturalness.

She could see that he hadn't quite believed her when she'd said she didn't want luxury, but now, here in this simple villa, with only themselves for company, he had realised she had been telling the truth. And he, too, seemed to be taking this simple life as natural for him.

Was it taking him back to his roots? she found herself wondering. Listening to him telling her about the work he was doing in his own country, to help others make a better life for themselves, about the difficulties they faced, the hopelessness so many lived with, even simply hearing him speak his mother tongue Spanish when they'd arrived on Majorca, had brought home to him just how different his background was from hers. How harsh his early years had been, and how much his life had changed since he was a teenager newly come to Britain, trying to make a new life for himself.

She longed to ask him about it—how he had coped with the trauma of settling in a new country, often hostile and indifferent to him. But she sensed a restraint about it and would not force it. She understood it, too, for she herself did not yet want to talk about her life in England—did not want to tell him about her grandmother, the loss of her mental powers, the non-stop care she needed now. It was too emotional, too sad…

And with a darkening in her heart she knew she *never* wanted to tell Leon about the danger her home was in—about what her father had done.

What he had made her do...

Instinctively she veered away from thinking about it. She had resolved that she would not let her father's poison taint this miraculous time with Leon and she would keep to that. Her thoughts were fierce.

He's got nothing to do with it! Nothing! I'm here with Leon because I want to be—because it's the most wonderful, miraculous thing that's ever happened to me!

It could not last. She knew that. Knew it with a tearing helplessness. This brief, blissful time was all she would have. Soon—all too soon, she knew—they must leave. Leon's busy, demanding life would take over again, and he would have to return to work. And she could not continue to abandon her grandmother as she was doing now. When this idyll ended she would go home—back to her life, back to her grandmother. Would nurse her and care for her until the end came. She would never leave her.

Not even for Leon.

'I'm truly sorry about this—I wish to God I didn't have to go—but it's not something I can deal with here. I'll be back tomorrow, I promise—and then we'll come right back to Santera. I'll make sure I can stay an extra week to make up for abandoning you now.'

Leon leant forward and kissed her reassuringly. Flavia did her best to appear reassured, but she felt the thread of unease unwind inside her further, even here in Palma, at the hotel Leon had checked her into to await his return the following day. The outside world had called to Leon, and he was having to respond to it. He hadn't told her what it was that summoned him, only that it was unavoidable, and she knew she had to believe him on that. Trust him. She knew, too, that a man like Leon Maranz would have a thousand calls on his time.

Her eyes shadowed. For herself, she had only one other rival for her time—but it was an overpowering one. One she would never turn her back on.

She still had not yet told Leon about her grandmother, for she had not wanted anything of the outside world to intrude on their private paradise. Not yet. When they were both back in England, when she was ready to let the outside world back in willingly, acceptingly, then and then alone would she tell Leon about the woman had always been the most important person in her life, and how Harford had always been the most important *place* in her life—her beloved home.

Part of her longed to tell him—longed to talk to him about her grandmother, about Harford—but part of her was reluctant. What if he asked her why, if her grandmother was so frail, she had come away with him as she had? And—far more difficult—how could she possibly tell him now about the ugly threat her father had made? How could she possibly confess how her father had blackmailed her into getting in touch with Leon?

When she thought about it an icy pool congealed in her stomach. What had happened between her and Leon had been so extraordinary, so wondrous, that she did not want to sully it in even the slightest way with any taint from her father's vile machinations. Oh, she *would* tell Leon about it—of course she would!—but not yet. Not yet...

Because it was all so new to her—this revelation of how wonderful it was to be with him! How transformed she was by him! She wished with all her heart that she had never met Leon through her father, that he had had nothing to do with him in any way at all. She wanted, now, to separate them totally.

But she did not know how or when. She only knew not yet...

Fears clutched at her, and unease threaded its disquieting skein through her nerves. She wished Leon was not going to London—however briefly. In his arms she felt those fears silenced—but on her own they plucked at her again, making her uncertain and fearful.

She must not let them surface. So she bade him goodbye, returning his ardent embrace on parting and he set off for the airport in a taxi, leaving her to while away the day in Palma.

She didn't really know what to do with herself, and the unease she had felt on parting from him intensified as she meandered through the morning. Everywhere she looked people seemed to be in couples, carefree and on holiday. She told herself not to be morbid and stupid, that Leon was coming back the next day.

Suppose he's delayed? Suppose his business takes longer than he thought it would? Suppose something else crops up he has to deal with? Suppose he has to fly off further afield...?

She tried to put the anxious thoughts out of her head, but still the sense of unease grew oppressively, disturbingly.

She headed back to the hotel. She would have a siesta in her room and pass the time that way.

When something roused her she was initially too groggy to tell what it was. She stirred dopily. Then, with a jolt, she realised it was her mobile beeping. She had received a text.

Leon!

Immediately she sat up, snatching the phone from her bedside, clicking on 'view message'.

As her eyes focussed on the words she froze.

It was not from Leon...

'I would point out—' Leon's voice was icy, barely leashing his anger '—that it was Lassiter who requested this meeting urgently. So why the hell isn't he here?'

'I'm really very, very sorry, Mr Maranz.' Alistair Lassiter's secretary sounded flustered down the line. 'But all I can say is that he left for the Far East this morning. At very short notice,' she finished, her tone attempting to be placating.

Leon's jaw tightened with angry exasperation. Why the *hell* had Lassiter gone overboard to get him back to London to hammer out the deal right now and then promptly disappeared to the other side of Asia?

'*Where* in the Far East?' he demanded of the hapless secretary.

'Mr Lassiter said his plans were fluid,' she replied uncertainly.

Leon rang off, his face dark. Lassiter was up to something. Had he tracked down a late-entry white knight in the Far East? Was he hopeful of better bail-out terms? Well, the deal Leon was offering was the only one he was going to offer Lassiter, whatever the man did. But in the meantime he'd torn himself away from Flavia, and it had *not* been what he'd wanted to do.

Flavia...

Her name resonated in his head, weaving between his synapses like a seductive, sensuous silken flame.

Flavia...

Emotion welled in Leon, washing away all tiresome thoughts of Alistair Lassiter. Focussing on the one person he wanted to think about.

Flavia.

He said her name again in his head, feeling a rush of wonder. She was everything he'd dreamt she might be—everything and much, much more! He had known from the first moment of seeing her that he desired her, but now—oh, now she fulfilled so much more than desire. There was a warmth to her, a sincerity, an ardour, and a passion that was like a bright, true flame. How he had ever worried that she might be the spoilt daughter of luxury he could not now imagine!

I can trust her—believe her—be happy with her...

Happy...

The word resonated in his head like a sweet note of music.

So simple a word. Yet how much it encompassed! This past week with Flavia had been unforgettable—as if his life had become something it had never been before. As if he had found something he had never found before...

Found *someone* he had never found before…

Someone to be happy with.

Happy for ever?

The question hovered tantalisingly, wonderingly. Dared he ask it?

Dared he answer it?

He stared ahead of him, unseeing of the wide expanse of his office, the high vista out over the City beyond that had taken him so many years of dogged work to achieve. He was seeing only Flavia, smiling at him, with all the warmth in her gaze that he could dream of. Holding out her arms for him…

With a start, he got to his feet. What was the point of him hanging around here in London any more? Out in Palma Flavia was waiting for him, and that was all he cared about. He would head back to Majorca, to Flavia, without delay. Waste not one more moment without her. And as for that question—the one he longed to answer—well, there would be time. All the time they needed together to answer it. There was no rush, no urgency. They would take as much time as they needed, being with each other, learning all there was to know about each other, finding all the happiness that lay between them.

His spirits high, on a rush of anticipation to be with Flavia again that very day, he went through to his PA's office and let her know he was leaving again. Would she book the earliest Palma flight possible for him? Then, taking his leave, he headed to the lift, phoning Flavia's mobile as he went. He couldn't wait to tell her he was on his way back to her. Couldn't wait to be with her again—take her in his arms again!

Impatiently, standing by the lift doors, he waited for her to pick up.

But instead the call went through to voicemail. Frowning momentarily, he stepped into the lift as the doors opened, and redialled once he was in the lobby downstairs.

Yet again it went to voicemail. Well, maybe she was in the hotel pool. He tried one more time, still got voicemail, and left a message, duplicating it in a text as well. Then, to be on the safe side, as he settled himself in the car taking him to the airport he phoned the Palma hotel direct.

'Phone up to Señorita Lassiter's room, please,' he instructed the desk clerk.

Her answer was apologetic. 'I'm so sorry, Señor Maranz, but Señorita Lassiter checked out of the hotel last night.' She paused, then said enquiringly, 'Will you be settling her bill?'

CHAPTER ELEVEN

RAIN was beating on the windowpanes, rattling the frame. Flavia had drawn the curtains; the bedside light was low. Her heart was gripped by a vice.

I should have been here—I should have been here.

The words of condemning reproach went round and round in her head as she sat by her grandmother's bed. The nurse had gone an hour ago, saying she would be on call to come back 'at any time' as she'd said tactfully to Flavia.

Flavia knew what that meant. Had known the moment she'd arrived, forcing herself to drive the strange hire-car from Exeter airport through the driving rain eastwards along the A30 into Dorset.

Had known the moment she'd phoned Mrs Stephens back from Palma.

'It's your grandmother...'

Guilt had struck instantly.

I should never have left her—never!

With her head she could tell herself all she liked that she might just as well have been in London, dancing attendance on her father, as out in a paradise she had never dreamt of— but guilt still clawed at her with pitiless talons.

To have been so selfish! To have thought nothing at all of simply disappearing off with Leon! Living out some kind of self-indulgent idyll just because...just because...

She felt the words twist inside her, trying to get out even

as she tried to crush them back in. But she couldn't hold them back.

Just because I've fallen in love with him...

The words sheered across her mind, forcing themselves into her consciousness, jolting through her like an electric shock. But it was a shock that she had to disconnect at the mains—right away. *Now.* It wasn't something she could give any time to at all! Not now—*not now*! Guilt stabbed at her yet again. Worse than ever.

How can I be thinking of myself now? How can it matter a jot, an iota, what my feelings for Leon are when I'm sitting by my grandmother's bed?

Watching her dying...

The vice clamped tighter around her heart, and she could feel her body rock slightly to and fro with anguish. Her hands were clasped around one of her grandmother's hands—hers so strong and firm, her grandmother's so thin and weak. Unmoving.

The pulse at her grandmother's wrist was barely palpable, her breathing light and shallow. The palliative care nurse who had been there when Flavia had arrived, breathless and stricken, had talked her through how the end would come, though she had not been able to say just when it would come.

'It might be tonight—or tomorrow—or a few days. But I doubt it will be longer,' she'd said, her eyes full of sympathy. 'She is easing away from life.'

Tears had filled Flavia's eyes, and she'd turned away, heart seizing. 'I should have been here!' she'd said, her voice muffled with emotion.

'It would have made no difference,' the nurse had said kindly.

Only that I would not have felt so guilty like this, Flavia thought as she sat now in her midnight vigil.

The last weeks of her grandmother's life and her granddaughter had been cavorting on a beach, immersed in a torrid love-affair, thinking only of herself! Caring only about herself! Not caring anything about her grandmother—the woman who had raised her, who loved her, who had always, *always* been there for her!

Yet when the end of her life had been approaching, her granddaughter had not been there for her—she had deserted her for her own selfish self-indulgence.

Guilt stabbed at Flavia again, and self-hatred.

If she had gone to Leon simply to save Harford, simply to ensure her grandmother could end her days in her own home, and every moment with him had been an ordeal, then she might not have felt like this! Then she might have justified her absence, told herself she'd only been doing it for her grandmother's sake.

Lie, lie, lie—

Every moment in Leon's arms had been a moment in paradise! Every hour of the days she'd spent with him had been for *her* sake—her own selfish, heedless sake—not her grandmother's! Even now, here, at her grandmother's deathbed, she was still thinking about him! Still aching for him and missing him, wanting to be with him!

Just because she'd fallen in love with him…

No! Don't think about that! It doesn't matter and it isn't important! Only this is important—now—with Gran—the last time on earth you'll be with her…

Silently, tears spilled from her eyes, wetting her cheeks. Her heart ached with sorrow and grief. She clutched her grandmother's hand as the life ebbed slowly from her, hour by hour, during the long reaches of the rainswept night. Keeping her last vigil at her side.

Leon was watching the rain. It was pounding down on the pavements far below, streaking down the plate glass windows of his office. Darkening the sky.

His mood was dark, too. Emotion swirled, opaque and turbid. A single thought burned in his brain.

Where is she?

Where had she gone—and why? *Why?*
What the hell has happened to her?

She had simply vanished—disappeared! The only communication he'd got back after all his non-stop voicemailing and texting had been a bare, curt message.

Leon, I have to go. Sorry. Urgent family matters.

That was it. Nothing more. Nothing since. Just nothing.

Frustration bit like a fanged snake. What the hell was going on? Where was she? Why was she not talking to him? What had happened? He didn't understand—he just damn well didn't understand!

Part of him was desperately trying to find an acceptable reason for her total silence. Maybe she was out of range again. Maybe her phone had broken, got lost, been stolen. But if that were so, he knew there was no reason why she shouldn't have got in touch with his office via another phone. He was not exactly anonymous! And he'd given his office explicit instructions to put her through any hour of the day or night.

But she hadn't got in touch. Hadn't communicated with him in any way whatsoever.

It was as if she no longer existed.

Or as if *he* didn't...

Emotion gripped at him again. Where the hell was she? What the hell had happened to her?

Why is she doing this to me?

That was the worst of all—the question that was like a kick in the guts, a knife in his lungs, stopping his breathing. There had to be a reason—a good one!—why she had disappeared. There just *had* to be...

For the thousandth time he reread the only clue he had—*'urgent family matters.'*

What urgent family matters?

The only family he knew about was her father, so did Flavia's disappearance have anything to do with Alistair Lassiter's sudden journey to the Far East? But why not tell him? Why simply cut him out of her life—cut him stone-dead? As if there were nothing at all between them!

Why is she doing this to me?

The question tore at him again. That was the heart of it! That was what was eating him alive. Flavia, who had been as close to him as a heartbeat, who clung to him in trembling ecstasy, hugged him in spontaneous affection, held his hand with absolute confidence and familiarity as they walked along, was now treating him as if he didn't exist! Her silence was deafening—devastating.

Frustration gripped him in its vice. How the *hell* could he find out where she was, why she had disappeared, what was damn well going on and why? As if cold gel oozed through his veins, he was chillingly conscious of just how little he knew about Flavia. Oh, they'd talked and talked at Mereden and Santera, talked about anything and everything—easily, naturally, as if they'd been doing it all their lives—but what they hadn't talked about had been their personal lives.

I thought there would be time for that—much more time!

Instead, all he'd ever told her had been the bare bones of where he'd grown up, how he'd come to Britain and found a way to make something of himself. And as for Flavia—what had she told him about herself?

Very little. They hadn't talked about her father, and apart from saying she lived in the West Country, she'd said nothing else. He frowned. The West Country covered a fair amount of territory. He'd already run a search under her name for everywhere west of Salisbury, but nothing had come up.

She could be anywhere! Anywhere!

He strode back to his desk, his mood black and bleak. Those turbid emotions swirled inside him again—part frustration, part anxiety. And one more emotion as well. He knew what it was—knew it but did not want to identify it. Did not want to name it.

But it was there all the same. Like a knife piercing into him.

Hurting him...

He sat down in his chair, closing his eyes. The pain sliced again.

I thought we were happy together. I thought we'd found something in each other that was special—binding us together. Making everything good between us.

That was what made her disappearance, her obdurate silence, so impossible to understand. That she could have gone from the warm, ardent, wonderful woman she'd been to someone who could just walk away without any desire to communicate with him, to let him know what was happening.

If she has things to deal with, I can understand that! I don't demand she comes back to me immediately. I don't expect her to cut out everything else from her life! I only want to understand what those calls on her are—to know she's all right...

It was the blankness that was destroying him. The impotence. He wanted to know where she was, discover what she was coping with and why.

Where is she?

The question rang again in his head, as unanswerable now as it had ever been.

Grimly, he got out his work. He'd been working like the devil, trying to drown out his emotions with hard labour. Give his teeming mind something to grip on to. At least he didn't have the business of whether or not to proceed with bailing out Lassiter to contend with. Alistair Lassiter had gone as silent as his daughter...

No. Don't think about either of them! Don't speculate pointlessly, frustratingly, about whether Flavia's disappearance has anything to do with her father. Just focus on something else—anything else.

But for all his harsh self-adjurations the only question he was interested in kept surfacing.

Where is she and how can I find her?

Then, like a gate opening in his mind, something struck him. Her passport.

She'd got her passport couriered to the airport so she could fly to Santera.

Couriered from where?

His hand moving faster than his mind, he seized up his desk phone. His instructions to his PA were immediate. The courier company the concierge at Mereden had put in touch with Flavia would know *exactly* where they had fetched her passport from.

He sat back. Relief filled him. Finally he could make a start on finding her...

Within the hour he had his answer. Five minutes later, anticipation leaping in him, having keyed in the address, he was staring at an aerial image on his computer screen of the house Flavia called home. His first reaction was immediate.

No wonder she prefers it to London!

It might not be the largest country house he'd seen, and it certainly wasn't what the British called a stately pile, but the substantial Georgian greystone dwelling was lapped by several acres of lawned gardens, girdled with woods and set amongst the fields and rolling hills of deep English countryside.

A little jewel of a place, he could see.

Is that where she is now?

For a moment longer he stared at the image, as if he might see Flavia suddenly appear, walking out of the house. Then, with a start, he reached for his phone, ready to dial the number that went with the address. He felt his spirits leap, buoyed by searing hope. In less than a moment she might be answering the phone, speaking to him—

His office door opened. Leon's hand froze. His PA was standing there, hovering and looking harassed.

'I'm so sorry to disturb you, but Mr Lassiter is in my office—' she said. 'He is asking to see you. I know he doesn't have an appointment, but...' Her voice trailed off and she looked uncomfortable.

Exasperation spiked in Leon. God, the man had lousy timing, all right! For an instant he felt like telling him to get lost, but then, with a steadying intake of breath, he subsided. OK, he might as well see the man. For all he knew Lassiter might have come here about Flavia.

Fear struck him. *Was* that why Lassiter was here? Had something happened to Flavia? Had she had an accident? A disaster?

Even before he'd nodded at his PA, Lassiter had walked in. His expression, Leon could see instantly, was not that of a man come to report bad news about his daughter. There was an air of confident jauntiness that immediately set Leon's teeth on edge. So did Lassiter's equally jaunty greeting, and the way he took a seat without being invited.

Leon's expression lost any sign of the alarm it had momentarily held, and darkened. 'We had an appointment,' he said icily, 'made at your insistence, for which I specifically flew back to this country—and you failed to show.'

Lassiter was unabashed. 'Yes, sorry about that, old chap,' he answered airily, sounding not in the least apologetic. 'I had to fly to the Far East.' He paused minutely. 'Bit of a turn-up for the books on my side, as it happens.'

He looked expectantly across at Leon, who remained blank-faced. Beneath his impassive expression, however, he was wishing Lassiter to perdition. The last thing he wanted was to have to focus on his bail-out proposal. All he wanted to do—urgently—was get his office to himself and phone Flavia's home. Impatience burned in him. But he crushed it down. Like it or not, Lassiter was here, and Leon would have to deal with him first.

Lassiter had pursed his lips. He was looking, Leon assessed, sleeker than usual. Smugger than he had been in their previous exchanges, when his predominant attitude had veered between ingratiating and blustering. Leon waited, irritation suppressed, for Lassiter to continue.

'Yes,' went on Lassiter, as though Leon had made some encouraging remark, 'looks like there's another interested party out in the Far East. Made me a *very* tempting offer, I must say.'

He looked expectantly across at Leon, whose impassive regard remained undented. Lassiter was doing nothing except wasting his time and increasing Leon's irritation.

'Very tempting,' Lassiter went on after a moment. He looked hard at Leon. 'They're not interested in taking any equity. Just offering me a generous line of credit for further expansion.'

'Then I can see the attraction for you,' agreed Leon.

Flavia's father went on staring, clearly trying to read Leon's reaction, and equally clearly taken aback by his statement of agreement.

'So you can see,' he went on, 'why I'm giving them serious consideration.'

'Yes, I can,' was all the response he got.

Leon's deliberate impassivity triggered Lassiter into showing his hand completely.

'So why would I accept *your* offer if I can avoid losing equity by taking this new one that's come up?'

'Why indeed?' Leon agreed again. Then, with a slight lift of his hand, as he was getting bored now, as well as irritated, he simply said, 'I thought I'd made it clear that my deal is the one we discussed. It won't change. If this new offer means you don't accept mine, so be it.'

He'd kept his tone neutral, and the flash of anger in Lassiter's pouched eyes at being unable to hustle Leon into renegotiating his proposal left him unmoved. Any turnaround by him would be on *his* terms, not Lassiter's, and if Lassiter had found another white knight abroad, with less stringent conditions, good luck to him. To his mind, to bail out Lassiter without the control that equity would afford would be financial madness——Lassiter would just squander any loans and continue unabated in his lucrative but exploitative African ventures.

His gaze rested, unimpressed, on Alistair Lassiter.

It's a miracle Flavia isn't like her father—

The thought formed in Leon's head as he levelled his gaze on Lassiter. Flavia's warm sympathy for his *pro bono* work in South America, and her heartfelt indignation at the economic exploitation so many people suffered, was a complete contrast to her father's callous attitude that profiteering out of the impoverished Third World was perfectly acceptable.

Thinking of Flavia made his eyes flicker automatically to the image on the computer screen—the beautiful house in the tranquil Dorset countryside that she lived in and called home. Was she there now? Would a single phone call put him back in touch with her at last? His eagerness to reach for his phone and do so was almost overwhelming. He just had to get rid of Alistair Lassiter first.

He sat back pointedly, indicating there was nothing more to debate. Then, both to expedite Lassiter's departure and because he had no wish for his relations with Flavia's father to be unpleasant just because he wouldn't budge on his rescue package, he said, his tone cordial enough, 'I wish you luck with your alternative offer, and I hope you get the business settled soon. There's a great deal of good value in the company—you hardly need me to tell you that—but I have my own ways of operating, and I always want to take equity.'

There. That was surely sufficiently conciliatory to give Lassiter a face-saving exit. As he finished speaking, for an instant he thought he saw another flash of anger in the fleshy face, but a moment later it was gone. In its place was a resumption of the smiling bonhomie that Leon was used to seeing.

'Well, old chap,' he replied, his manner bland once more, 'I'm sorry you're going to let go the opportunity I've offered you, but there it is. Looks like the other lot get the deal.' He made it sound as though it were Leon's loss, and he got to his feet as if regretfully.

As he did so, he nodded towards the computer screen

on Leon's desk, and Leon realised, to his annoyance, that Lassiter must have been able to see it.

'Ah, I see you're taking a look at Harford. Beautiful place, isn't it? Flavia's devoted to it. Comes to her from her mother's side.' He smiled, as if jovially. 'But of course you'll know all that by now, won't you?'

There was a knowing look in his eyes, but Leon would not be drawn. His personal relationship with Flavia was not something he would discuss with her father.

Lassiter's expression lost its smile. 'Of course,' he went on, shaking his head, his voice rueful, 'sadly—like so many of these upper-crust county families—they ran out of money some time ago. That's why, if I'm absolutely honest about it,' he confided, 'Flavia's mother was so ready to snap me up— self-made as I am. Because I could help finance its upkeep. I still do. It's cost me a fortune over the years, but Flavia adores the place—would do anything to keep it.' He paused. 'Anything at all.'

He smiled. Paused again. 'She's a lovely girl, isn't she? So beautiful! I could tell you were very taken with her, and I'm glad you've got together now, despite her being...well, a bit capricious towards you initially. I don't like to say such things, as a fond father, so you must allow me some prejudice in her favour. I can never see any wrong in her—but that's fathers for you!'

He smiled again, dotingly. 'Her mother was just like her— beautiful and determined. She always knew what she wanted! And how to get it!' He gave a little laugh—an indulgent one. 'Mind you, she could be sweet as pie, too—when she was after something!' Now he looked Leon in the eyes again, an open, frank expression on his face. 'I never thought I stood a chance of winning her—I've never been a handsome chap— but I did at least have money to my name. Some people might say it was wrong of her to take that into account, but I could never hold it against Flavia's mother. She was just as devoted to Harford as her daughter is, and she wanted to save it any way she could—it's very understandable. *Very* understandable.'

He gave a sigh. 'When she set her cap at me because she knew I could preserve Harford for the family she was just too beautiful to resist—I was putty in her hands. And when she died, so tragically young—well, I guess it's not surprising I lavished everything on our daughter.' He shook his head regretfully. 'And I guess it's not surprising that it meant Flavia grew up thinking she could have everything she wanted. I know she can be moody—' there was an apologetic note to his voice '—well, you saw that for yourself, didn't you, at the charity ball?' he acknowledged. 'But I made allowances that evening because I knew how worried she was about my state of affairs.' He held up a hand. 'Not that I've burdened her with them. I would never do that! But she's a smart girl, and must have got wind of how things stood with me.'

He nodded at the image on the computer screen again. 'She'll be *so* pleased you've taken an interest in Harford, I know. Have you been there yet with her?' he asked. 'Mind you, now that you and I won't be business partners after all things may change on that front. It wouldn't surprise me, I have to say. But if you should go down, you'll see why Flavia's so devoted to it and how much she wants me to be able to keep it safe for her—expensive luxury though it is.'

He started towards the door. 'Well, I mustn't keep you. We're both very busy men. I'm sorry we shan't be partners, but of I look forward to seeing more of you with Flavia on the social front,' he answered Leon. 'If the two of you are still together, of course.'

He opened the door and was gone.

At his desk, Leon sat very, very still. Then, slowly, he reached for his phone to make his call to Flavia.

He had one very simple question to ask her.

CHAPTER TWELVE

'EARTH to earth, ashes to ashes…'

The rector's voice was low and resonant. Flavia stood, head bowed, tears running down her cheeks. Her grandmother would lie beside her husband in her grave, as together in death as they had been through all their long married life. Grief buckled through her again, as it had been doing over and over again in the long days and the longer nights since her grandmother's breathing had become shallower and shallower…and then stopped completely.

The committal ended and she lifted her head, blinking away her tears, knowing she now had to get through the ordeal of a reception at Harford for the mourners to attend. It was what her grandmother would have wanted, but she felt she couldn't take one more expression of sympathy, one more person calling the loss of her beloved grandmother a '*merciful release*' before adding '*and not just for your grandmother*' with an encouraging expression on their faces.

One person had even said right out, 'It was no life for you here, buried in the countryside at your age—a young girl— no life at all. You should have been off living your own life. finding romance and excitement.'

Anger and guilt had pierced her, needle-sharp, lancing in and out of the ravening grief that shook her, body and mind. It was like being possessed, blocking out everything else.

Even thinking about Leon.

No! She mustn't think about Leon—not now—not yet. He belonged to a different world—a world she wasn't in right now. She had to blank it out totally because she couldn't cope with it. Even without the guilt spearing her she couldn't have coped with that world now. *With* the guilt, it was impossible!

I should have been here, with my grandmother—I should never have gone off with Leon!

It was no good telling herself that at least she had come back in time to be with her grandmother at the very end— no good telling herself that her grandmother would not even have realised she had gone away.

And no good telling herself, with chill bleakness, that she had done what she had in order to save Harford for her grandmother.

Numbly, she somehow got through the reception, played the role of dutiful granddaughter even though she had betrayed her grandmother at the last, putting herself first, her own desires...

Indulging herself with Leon, and all that he'd offered her.

But she couldn't bear to think of Leon, because guilt racked her on his account as well. She'd abandoned him to rush back to her grandmother, and knowing she had done so crushed her with guilt, too.

Guilt...every way she turned. Guilt over her grandmother for not being with her, guilt over the reasons she'd gone to Leon at her father's malign bidding, then yet more guilt for abandoning him to rush back home again...

The guests were all gone at last, and she finished clearing up after them. She wandered blindly outside, looking back at the house. Never again would she see her grandmother here. Never.

The word tolled in her head and she felt her heart squeeze with grief. The future stretched ahead—a future she would have to cope with somehow. Dealing with probate, with the aftermath of death. She took a shuddering breath. Dealing somehow with what was going to happen to Harford.

The burden of her father's loan still hung like an ugly weight over her head, and now death duties would strike, too. Could Harford survive them both? Anxiety pressed at her. Her plans for the time when her grandmother would be no more had been laid long ago. She would raise a mortgage on Harford and use the money to pay off death duties, pay the mortgage off slowly by turning the house and any outbuildings she could afford to convert into upmarket holiday lets.

Now, though, she would have to raise enough to pay off her father as well. On that she was determined. Her father would be out of her life. Out for good! And when she was finally free of him…

She felt a rush of blood, of longing.

When I'm free of my father—finally, finally free!—then and only then can I be free to seek out Leon again. To see if the magic is still there, to see if that wonderful, blissful time with him can be recaptured. But pure this time, clean and free of any taint by my father!

The power of her longing almost overcame her. To be able to go to Leon without deceit, without pressure, without the malign, corrupting influence of her father. She would offer herself as she truly was, without any of her father's venal agenda, with no hidden motive, no shameful collusion to further her father's interests, no guilt-racked obligations to her grandmother to save her house by any means she must— whatever it took.

Shame flushed through her again at what she had done. Oh, she would have willingly—*so* willingly!—gone to Leon, given herself up to that overpowering response to him she had felt the moment she'd first set eyes on him, had she not had her responsibility to her grandmother, the duty of love for her, to hold her back. Yet even with that knowledge the taint of her father's scheming still haunted her. Even though she knew that she would have done what she had, rejoiced as she had, embracing the time she'd had with Leon, it still had the sleazy shadow of her father's ultimatum to her louring over it.

But now—now she could finally free herself of that sleazy shadow. Now she could pay off her father—free herself for ever from his baleful influence over her life.

Free herself to focus only on what she so deeply longed for. Leon.

I want him so much. I miss him so much.

Like a beacon shining through the pall of her grief for her grandmother, the malign shadow of her father, her longing for Leon called to her.

And now I can go to him. Free—free of my duty of love to my grandmother, free of my father's hideous threats. Free to go to Leon only as myself, what I am, what I truly am...

Hope flared in her and she lifted her bowed head, looking afresh out over the gardens of the house she loved. Resolution filled her, and hope for the future—longing for the man who had opened to her a world of wonder she had never dreamt could be hers.

And it could be hers again...

Memory, rich and golden, glowed in her vision. The starlit terrace at Mereden, the river flowing beyond the lawns stretching away from them, Leon's hands cupping her face, his mouth seeking hers. The warm, cicada-filled nights on Santera, clinging to Leon, her body trembling in ecstasy.

Just being with him! Walking along the little sandy beach among the fragrant pine trees, barefoot, hand in hand. Laughing with him as they made their nightly barbecues. Curled up against him on the sun lounger as they took their daily siesta in the baking heat of the day. Breakfasting with him over coffee and pastries in the cool of the morning, with the little breeze fresh off the water's edge.

Just her and Leon. Easy. Happy. Blissful.

Yearning filled her—an ache in her heart for him...only him...

She took a deep, steadying breath. Her mind raced ahead. Tomorrow she would see the solicitors, get probate moving as swiftly as she could. She would visit the bank manager, too, to set in motion her plans for raising a mortgage, getting liquid funds to pay off her father's pernicious, punishing loan. Plan ahead for readying Harford for the holiday let market in the spring.

And, most precious of all, tomorrow she would write to Leon.

I'll tell him everything! Everything! About my grandmother, how I had to abandon him as I did because she was dying. About my vile father, how he threatened Harford, and how I had to protect it for my grandmother's sake. I will confess everything to him—confess what I dared not tell him before—and beg his understanding, his forgiveness!

As she stood there in the warm summer air, gazing out over the lawns streaked with the last of the afternoon's sun, for the first time since she had rushed back to her dying grandmother's side she felt hope surge through her. Yes, she would grieve for her grandmother, accept her guilt for abandoning her as she had, accept her shame for the way she had had to capitulate to her father, but for all that she would not give up on Leon—she would strive to recapture the bliss they had shared. Make all things right with him.

Make a future with him.

Her heart squeezed with longing.

Oh, please, please let it be so! Let there be a future with him—I long for him so much. So much!

As she stood and felt the emotion of her longing for him seize her, her hope for a future with him sear within her, gazing out over the gardens of the home she loved so much, she became aware of a disturbance in the peaceful tranquillity of the air. A distant, rhythmic throbbing that grew louder and louder still.

She looked up, craning her neck, into the sky. It was a helicopter, its rotors chopping the air like a fearful heartbeat. She stared, hearing and then seeing the machine loom over the trees beyond, coming from the east. A frown warped her brow as she watched it descend. Heading down towards the lawn.

The branches of the trees at the edge of the lawn were whipping frenziedly in the gusts, the tall flowers in the herbaceous borders were winnowed, the grass below the machine flattened. Before her eyes the helicopter landed, setting down on the wide lawn beyond the terrace. Its engines were cut. The whirling, thudding vanes slowed. They had hardly stopped when the door opened and a tall, lithe figure jumped down.

Like a flame leaping inside her, Flavia felt her heart sing out.

Leon! It was Leon!

Leon—here—now. Come to her.

Disbelieving with joy, she could only stand, watching him walking towards her, her heart full.

As he alighted from the helicopter Leon could feel his heart churning. The rhythmic chopping of the helicopter's rotors was still throbbing in his head. Even before the machine had landed he had seen Flavia standing there in front of the house—the gracious, greystone Georgian house that was every bit as beautiful as it had looked on the computer screen, every bit as beautiful as Alistair Lassiter had said it was.

No wonder Flavia Lassiter wanted to hang on to it.

Just as her father had said.

He could hear him talking again in his head, hear what he'd said about her. The words fell like stones. Destroying, one by one, everything Leon had thought he knew about Flavia…

The knife that those words had plunged into his side twisted again.

The moment Lassiter had gone out of his office Leon had seized up the phone, called the number on his screen. Urgency had impelled him—but a new urgency.

No one had picked up the phone. All he had got was an answer-machine, telling him to leave a message. He'd dropped the phone down. No, he would *not* leave a message. He would not wait pointlessly for Flavia *not* to return his call, just as she hadn't any of his calls. The time for that was over. It was time for something much more decisive.

He straightened, seeing her standing there, stock still, on a gravelled terrace on the far side of the lawn the helicopter had landed on. The churning in his heart intensified, his emotions firing like gunshots. As his eyes rested on her, he could hear a silent cry come from him.

Flavia!

Flavia standing there—as beautiful as his memory had painted so vividly—real and close and there in front of him. He wanted to rush up to her, sweep her into his arms, fold her close against him! Feel her heart beating against his!

But instead all he did was quicken his stride towards her, feeling the knife in his side strike again.

I have to know! I have to know whether she's the way her father says she is or whether...

Whether she was the woman he had discovered that night at Mereden, those magical days and nights on Santera. Passionate and ardent. Warm, genuine, sympathetic, generous.

Or someone quite different. Someone who could be as sweet as you like when she wanted something. Someone who set her sights on something and went after it, whatever it required.

Such as deliberately, calculatingly having an affair with a man she thought was going to bail out her father—the father who was keeping her home solvent.

Again, as it had done over and over on the journey here, the question seared in his head. *Was it true—was it true what her father had said of her?*

The knife twisted in his guts again.

His stride quickened and he reached the terrace. For an instant longer Flavia seemed to stand there, transfixed. Then...

'Leon! Oh, Leon!'

She had thrown herself at him, and without conscious volition his arms went around her. Held her to him. Closed around her. Emotion clenched in him. It seemed a lifetime since he had last seen her, last kissed her as he boarded the flight for London, leaving her behind in Palma. But now she was back in his arms, her face buried in his shoulder. Almost, *almost* he forgot what had sent him here, heart churning, thoughts dark as night. Almost he simply cupped her face and kissed her lips with his, recapturing the happiness he'd felt with her.

Almost.

But then, with a ragged breath, he steeled. Put her away from him. She swayed, gazing at him, the joyous expression draining out of her face. Bewilderment, consternation took its place. Leon wanted to seize her back into his arms, make her eyes shine again—but he forced himself to resist.

Not yet—not yet. First he *must* know the answer to the question he would demand of her.

I thought I knew her—had discovered the real Flavia beneath the freezing exterior.

But if that were a fiction—a lie? What if the damning portrait her father had painted at was true? What if Flavia had been running a play the whole time they were together?

The knife in his side twisted again.

He looked about him. Looked down the length of the perfectly proportioned Georgian façade flanked by gardens. *Oh, yes, this place was a jewel, all right!*

'So,' he said slowly, 'this is Harford.'

His gaze came back to her. She was standing, had paused, consternation still in her face, but there was something new, too—a tension netting about her. A wariness.

'How...how did you find it?' she faltered.

Her first joy at seeing Leon—the rush of pleasure in running into his arms—had gone. When he had put her aside it had been like a douche of cold water. Now she realised that she had no idea how it was he came to be here.

He doesn't know anything about Harford! Doesn't even know it exists, let alone that I live here!

Yet here he was, standing right in front of her. And with an expression on his face that was sending cold all the way through her.

'The courier company you used to fetch your passport gave me the address,' he said.

His voice was distant. Dark eyes rested on her. She could not read their expression, and that of itself made the chill in her veins deepen.

'Why didn't you tell me about Harford, Flavia? Why the big secret?'

She swallowed. 'I...I was going to tell you,' she began, then could go no further.

'But you didn't, did you? Did you think it would scare me off?'

Before his doggedly impassive gaze he could see a dull flush stain her face. Revealing to him that he had hit home.

The knife twisted in him again.

His eyes swivelled away—it seemed easier than watching her colour in front of him, betraying herself. He looked about him.

'It's a gem of a place,' he said slowly. It was, too—a flawless example of a miniature country house, at one with its landscaped gardens, a beautiful, peaceful haven from the world.

He thought of his own upbringing in the fetid, rat-infested *favela*—an ocean away from here! Oh, Flavia Lassiter came from a different world—a different universe! Bitterness filled him, and anger, and a deep, numbing cold that iced all the way through him.

All masked an emotion that went much, much deeper. That bored into him with every twist of that knife in his side.

Flavia was speaking, her voice low and faltering. He made himself listen, made his gaze go back to her, though her image seemed to burn on his retinas. Her beauty assaulted him. She was dressed as soberly as she had been in London: her narrow skirt black, her neat high-necked blouse lavender, a jet brooch at the collar, her hair back in its chignon, her face bereft of make-up. There were dark circles under her eyes, he noted with a strange pang, as if she were not sleeping well.

He thrust the observation aside, making himself listen to what she was saying so haltingly. Was she trying to find words to counter that revealing flush? Was that it? His jaw tightened.

'...so sorry. I'm so very sorry I left you like that. But—'

He held up a hand, silencing her. 'I understand the reason,' he said.

Urgent family matters—and now he knew just what those were...

She looked puzzled. 'You do?'

'Yes. It's very simple, after all.' His voice was expressionless. 'You didn't bother to wait for me in Palma because by then you knew there was no need to. Your father had already contacted you about the new white knight he'd flown off to have discussions with. So there was no reason to hang around with me any more, was there? It wasn't *me* who was going to save his skin—or this place. So you could dispense with me—which you very promptly did.'

She had gone pale. White as a sheet. Leon could feel his emotions lash through him like the tip of a whip.

'*What?*'

Her astonishment was convincing. Very convincing.

But not to him. It only made him angry—like a wounded jaguar.

'Are you going to try and deny it?' he retorted.

'Yes! Of course I am!'

'And what else are you doing to try and deny?'

'What do you mean?' Her voice was hollow, strained.

'Tell me—what was my main attraction to you, Flavia? What made you stop totally ignoring my calls and get in touch with me? Accept my invitations?' He paused. A deadly pause. 'Have an affair with me...?'

Her eyes were wide, so wide, as she made herself answer. Emotion was storming through her. Making it hard to speak. Impossible to think.

'Because...because I couldn't say no to you...'

Leon's gaze speared her. 'Really? Or because you couldn't *risk* saying no to me…'

That flush came again—a fateful, betraying dull flaring of colour staining her cheekbones. Staining her conscience.

'I have to explain.' It was a whisper. A plea.

'Do you? I don't see why. Your father gave me all the explanation I need.' His voice was chill.

Her expression stilled. 'What did my father say to you?'

Now it was her voice that was chill. Leon's face hardened. 'He said quite a lot.'

Flavia's chin lifted. A cold pit had formed in her stomach. 'What did he tell you?'

What lies has he fed you—and why are you believing them?

She wanted to shout the words at him—but the cold inside her was taking over, freezing through her veins. Paralysing her.

Leon's level gaze never left her face. 'He said that you were determined to hang on to this place—whatever you had to do to keep it.'

She opened her mouth, then closed it again. Leon's eyes were like the talons of a hawk, tearing into her. Cruel and pitiless.

He was speaking again, and she had to force herself to hear him through her faintness.

'You wanted to keep me sweet so I would be likely to bail out your father. Until your father told you he didn't need me any more—then you didn't either. So you left me.'

She shook her head violently. 'No! *No*—Leon—listen. That wasn't why I left!'

She stepped forward, as if to cling to him, but his hands closed over her elbows like a vice. Holding her away from him. His face was dark like thunder.

'Don't lie to me!'

'Leon—listen to me—*please*!'

'No—*you* listen to *me*. I have one question—*one question*—and it's a very simple one.' His eyes skewered into hers, like stakes. 'Did you or did you not finally answer my calls to you and agree to go out with me because I was going to rescue your father's company? Just tell me the truth—yes or no?'

Her mouth opened—then closed. Her face worked.

'Leon, I have to *explain*—' She tried to speak but her throat was closed, stricken. Guilt and shame washed through her.

He thrust her back, letting her go, and she swayed.

'No.' His voice was cold, and hard as steel. 'You *don't* have to explain. Was it to save this place that you came to me? Because I was going to bail out your father? Yes or no?'

'Leon—please, *please*—'

'You don't deny what I've asked—that means it's true. Isn't it? *Isn't it*?'

She could feel her teeth start to chatter. 'Leon, please...' Her voice was a whisper again, forced out past the agonisingly tight cords of her throat.

His hands on her elbows was like a vice. 'Tell me it isn't true. Just tell me that. Yes—no. Very, very simple.'

Her face was working. She was trying to speak. But she was powerless to do so. Powerless to give the answer she so desperately wanted to give him...

'Yes or no?' His voice was remorseless, his face implacable. *'Yes or bloody no, Flavia?'*

'I...I...' She could get no further. Her eyes were anguished, guilt and shame convulsing her.

Something changed in his face. 'Your silence gives me the answer.' His voice was dead. He dropped his grip on her.

'Leon, *please*—let me explain—' She reached a hand towards him—begging. She had to find a way—she had to tell him, explain...confess.

But he'd turned away from her, was walking away from her. She watched him go—helpless, stricken. At the edge of the lawn he paused, looking back at where she stood, frozen.

'There's a word for you, Flavia, for what you did. What you were prepared to do.' He looked around him again for a moment, taking in all the tranquil beauty of the house and its sun-filled gardens, then back at her, his gaze slicing her open, lacerating her. 'And it doesn't matter whether you were doing it to try and save this place, because whatever justification you try and come up with the answer is the same. The name for you is the same.'

He paused, and took a ragged, razored breath. 'I would have given you the world—all I possessed. What we had...' He paused again, then forced the words out. 'What I thought we had was—'

He broke off. Then wordlessly he turned, and strode out across the lawn, back into the waiting helicopter.

The rotors started to turn.

Like a giant bird of prey it lifted off into the air.

Leaving her carrion carcass far below.

Somehow—she didn't know how—Flavia stumbled indoors. Got herself inside her bedroom and threw herself down on her bed. Distraught, fevered sobs seemed to crack her ribs and rack her throat, convulse her whole body.

How long they lasted she didn't know—couldn't tell. She only knew that when they had finally emptied her out she could only lie there, staring at the ceiling, feeling as drained and hollowed out as an empty husk of rotten fruit.

Facing the truth. The bitter, shaming truth.

Leon had every right to accuse her—every right to despise her.

I should have told him the truth! I should have told him on Santera just what my father had done!

But she had been too ashamed to do so. Too fearful that Leon would despise her—too fearful that if he'd rejected her for what she'd stooped to then her father would have carried out his threat and taken Harford from her grandmother...

And fearful for more than that. Much, much more. As she lay, staring, tear-stained, up at the white blank ceiling, she faced the truth within her.

I was scared he would reject me for what I'd done—hate me for it. Hate me just when I was falling in love with him...

And now the truth had come out and he had done what she had feared so much. Thrust her from him, despising and condemning her.

And there was nothing she could do about it—because it was true. The truth had condemned her...

I've lost him and I can do nothing to win him back. Nothing. He's condemned me—rejected me.

Despair filled her.

He hates me now—he hates me and there's nothing I can do to make him not hate me. Because what he accused me of is true.

She could tell herself all she liked that she had had no choice but to collude with her father or he would have forced her grandmother to lose her home—that still didn't take away what she had done to Leon. Deceived him and betrayed his trust in her.

In her head, anguished, she heard his voice, low and intense—*'I would have given you the world...'*

She closed her eyes, feeling wave after wave of pain wash over her, crying his name in her head.

On leaden limbs she dragged herself up, forced herself to go downstairs. Out in the garden, the sun had long gone, and twilight was gathering in the shadows. Limply she sat down on a bench looking out over the silent lawns. How often had she seen her grandparents, sitting here, hand in hand, looking out over the gardens? They had loved each other deeply. With needle pain she envied them with all her heart.

Now they were both gone, and only she was left. She had lost them, one by one, and now she had lost the man she knew she loved.

She did not cry—there were no tears left to weep. Instead she heard a small, anguished voice inside her cry out.

What am I to do—what am I to do?

And as she sat it was as if she could hear inside her head the calm, wise voice of her grandmother.

'When you wrong someone, child, you must put it right.'

She gazed out over the place she loved most on earth. The place she had tried to protect for her grandmother's sake. But her grandmother did not need her home any more.

The cry from her heart pierced Flavia.

But I need it! I need it—I love it so much and it's all I have left! I've lost everything else—only this is left to me! Only this!

Yet the voice in her head came again. *'You must put it right, child—whatever it costs you. Then and only then can your conscience be clear again.'*

Wind winnowed the hairs at the back of her neck. A last songbird called from the high bushes. The scent of roses caught at her.

'You must put it right, child...'

She closed her eyes, hearing her grandmother's voice, bowing her head. A strange kind of peace filled her. Then slowly, very slowly, she got to her feet and went back indoors. She had wronged Leon. And she had lost him. But she *would* put it right—the only way she could.

In her head his voice sounded again. *'I would have given you the world...'*

She did not have the world—but she knew what it was she must give *him*.

CHAPTER THIRTEEN

'THERE you go, Mrs Peters. That's more comfortable, isn't it?'

Flavia's voice was cheerful, and she smiled down at the elderly lady in her bed, whose pillows she had just rearranged, even though Mrs Peters only went on staring ahead of her blankly. But that didn't stop Flavia chatting away to her as she tended her the way she had her grandmother. Carefully she brushed her patient's hair, gave her some sips from the glass of barley water on the bedside table, which Mrs Peters took docilely, if wordlessly.

Her tasks done for the moment, Flavia bade her patient a kindly leavetaking, and went out of the room. Time to look in on her next charge.

It wasn't difficult work, though seeing elderly women so similar to her grandmother could make her heart ache with loss at times, but it took energy, and patience, and endless cheerfulness, and a great deal of kindness and consideration to look after her charges. Given all her experience caring for her grandmother, it had seemed the obvious work for her to do, and the job also had the huge benefit of providing live-in accommodation at a residential care home.

Just how long she would go on working here she wasn't sure—she couldn't think very far ahead yet. It was enough simply to have a steady job and something useful to do each day.

And to be far, far away from everywhere and everything she'd known. And everyone.

It was what she wanted. All that she could do right now. To get right away from her past and leave it all behind her. Eventually, she knew, she would feel strong enough to lift her head up from the daily round and try and think what to do with the rest of her life.

But that time hadn't come yet, and in the meantime this was enough.

She was just about to go into the next room on the corridor when one of the other carers spotted her.

'Oh, there you are. Someone phoned, asking about you.'

Flavia froze. *What on earth...?*

Apart from her grandmother's solicitors, no one knew she was here. Her eyes hardened. If her father were trying to contact her, using them to do so, he would not succeed. She would have nothing to do with him ever again. On that she was adamant. She was free of him now, and he would never harm or injure her again.

Not that he'd made any attempt to contact her before. She'd presumed he'd accepted he had no more hold over her and therefore he could not use her for his own purposes again. So she had ceased to exist for him. What he was up to these days she neither knew nor cared. Presumably Leon had bailed him out, and he was merrily sporting Anita—or her successor—wherever he wanted to be.

She walked down to the office and went inside.

'Did they leave any message?' she asked.

The other carer—Maria—shook her head. 'They just wanted to know if you worked here,' she told Flavia.

Flavia stiffened. 'Did you tell them?'

'Yes.' The other woman nodded. 'Shouldn't I have?'

Flavia gave a quick smile. 'No, that's fine—don't worry.'

But behind the smile she was frowning. Who could it have been if not her father?

She could feel her heart convulse. Heard a name leap in her head. Immediately she crushed it down.

It isn't Leon! He won't get in touch! I know he won't! He's got no reason to—none at all!

She would never see him again. She knew that. Accepted it. Had made herself accept it.

It's over—completely over. I treated him shamefully and though I have tried to make amends, it cannot be mended. Because I can't undo what I did to him. My father pimped me to him and I went along with it. It doesn't matter why I did it—I did it. So all our time together was a lie! How could it have been anything else?

Anguish filled her. Well, she'd been punished for what she'd done. Punished in a way she had never foreseen. With a perfection of justice that was exquisite in its torment.

I went to him at my father's bidding and my punishment was to fall in love with him—and for him to know what I'd done and hate me for it...

She was in love with a man who had every reason to hate her and despise her, and that was something she would have to live with from now on. Until surely, she prayed, love withered and died. For it must eventually—it must wither and die without nurture, without hope.

I made amends in the only way I could and I have to leave it at that. I have to.

She took a razored breath, setting off back down the corridor to go on with her work. As she tended her next charge, washing and bathing her, helping her into fresh clothes, settling her comfortably once again, she almost she found herself envying her patients' dissociation from the world. Wherever their minds were, they did not have to deal with the emotions that knifed through her so tormentingly. They had gone beyond emotion—gone beyond love...

Beyond loss.

Her hours at work passed swiftly enough, for there was never a shortage of things to do. It was a good care home,

Flavia knew, but seeing its inmates she also knew, with absolute conviction and certainty, that her grandmother would have hated it—however good the quality of care. She had only been contented at Harford—knowing somewhere in the depths of her silent mind that she was at home. Safe.

The knowledge was another layer of torment in the vortex that twisted constantly in her heart now.

I could only keep Gran at Harford by doing what I did to Leon—there was no other way. No other way.

But, whatever the motive, the deed was the same. Shaming her. Damning her.

So I have to pay the price without complaint, without self-pity.

'Flavia!'

The sound of her name broke her reverie of misery. She looked up. Matron was beckoning her. Dutifully, Flavia went over to her.

'You've got a visitor,' Matron said. 'Usually I don't allow such things in working time, but on this occasion I will make an exception.'

There was the slightest ruffled look about her normally brisk manner, but before Flavia could speculate, Matron was ushering her inside her own inner sanctum, which she hadn't been in since her original job interview nearly four months ago. But she had hardly got inside the doorway before she stopped dead. Frozen.

Leon was inside.

Her first reaction was disbelief, followed by a storm of emotions. She fought for control, clinging to the door handle for stability.

How on earth had he found her?

Had she spoken out loud? She must have, for he was answering her, his face set.

'I bullied your solicitor into telling me.'

'Why?'

'Because he wouldn't tell me willingly,' he replied tersely.

Flavia shook her head as if to clear it. 'No, I mean *why* did you want to know?'

Emotion flashed in his eyes. 'You ask *why*? Did you think I wouldn't want to track you down—find you—after your solicitors had been in touch with me?'

She was trying to get control back but her mind was all to pieces. She was speaking without thinking, without conscious volition. All her consciousness was on Leon's presence here.

So close...

Every sense was leaping in her body, overwhelming her. *I thought I'd never see him again.*

But he was here—now—dragging her gaze to him so he dominated her vision, and she could see nothing else at all except Leon. She could feel her heart going like a sledgehammer, her legs weak with shock. With more than shock.

His face was stark, his cheekbones etched like knives.

'You gave me Harford.'

His words fell into the silence. A silence she could not break. She could only stand there frozen, immobile, incapable of speech, or thought, or anything at all other than a reeling of her mind that he was here. Leon was here...

'Why?' His question bit into the air. 'Why did you do it, Flavia?'

She took a ragged breath. 'I had to do it.'

His face darkened. But she did not let him speak.

'I had to do it because it was the only thing I *could* do. All I could think to do.' She took another shuddering breath, her eyes anguished. 'To try and make amends to you for what I did. For deceiving you. Using you. I behaved unforgivably— I know I did. And I am more sorry for my behaviour than you can ever know.' She could hear her voice catch dangerously, and knew she had to plunge on. 'Gifting Harford to you seemed to me all I could do to attempt to make amends,' she said awkwardly. 'It wasn't actually much of a gift, because of the debts on the property, but I knew you would clear something once they'd all been paid, and…and I didn't have anything else to give you.'

'Debts?' His voice was blank.

'Yes. I knew the taxman would want his share for death duties.' She took a difficult breath. 'And that the other claimant would have to be paid back, too.'

His dark eyes were levelled on her. Still expressionless. She bore their weight pressing down on her, trying not to collapse beneath it. She could feel the pulse at her throat throbbing.

Why had he come here? What for? She'd done what she could—all that she could!—to show him how much she regretted what she'd done to him at her father's behest. So why had he tracked her down. Just to get her to spell it out to him like this?

'The other claimant?' His words echoed hers, but heavily, like stones. He paused. 'You mean, of course, your father?'

Her lips pressed together again. 'Yes, my father. I'm sorry about that, Leon, because it was a vast amount of money I owed him. But there was nothing I could do. The loan agreement was watertight. I had it checked, and there was no way I could get out of having to repay that final sum because of the rate of interest.'

'The one set by your father?' The same blank, heavy voice. She nodded, swallowing. 'Yes. I'm sorry.'

'You're sorry?'

He seemed to be echoing everything she said—echoing it as if each word weighed a ton.

'Of course I'm sorry! That debt to him ate into the value of the house hideously.'

'Yes, it did.' He paused, and she felt the world still for a moment. Then he spoke again. His voice sounded distant, remote. 'One might wonder,' he said, 'just why your father should have set such a rate of interest in the first place. Considering the loan was to his mother-in-law.'

'He didn't care for her,' said Flavia.

'So one might surmise, from the terms and conditions of

the loan,' Leon commented. 'Had she done something to injure him that he set such terms?'

'No,' she answered. 'But there was no love lost between
them.'

'Evidently.' Leon's voice was dryer than the Sahara. 'And
yet one might think it reasonable to suppose—' his voice
was deadpan now '—that once his own daughter had inherited Harford that ruinous debt would be instantly lifted. Why
would he want his own daughter to owe him money like that?
What father would want that? What *devoted, loving* father?
Because he is devoted to you, Flavia—he's told me so himself! Several times! So devoted, he assured me, it was *his*
money that kept Harford afloat!'

She didn't answer. Couldn't. His eyes were like weights
on her, crushing her into the ground.

'Except that it didn't, did it? In fact it almost sank like a
stone. That debt was hanging round your neck like a lead
weight! The house you'd inherited after the death of your
grandmother—who *died*, Flavia, forty-eight hours after you
left Palma, whose funeral was the day I confronted you at
Harford after what your father had told me—'

His voice was no longer dry. It was no longer expressionless. It was filled with a black, murderous rage.

'You,' he bit out, 'are now going to tell me the truth! Finally and comprehensively. And you are *not* going to escape
this—do you understand me? Because I have been through
months of *hell* trying to find you, and I will not go through
one more hour! Not *one*!'

She was staring wide-eyed, stricken. 'Leon, please...' Her
voice was strained, low-pitched. 'I've done what I can to make
amends—it's all I can do. I did what I did and I can't undo
it. I know it was unforgivable, and I hate myself for it, but
giving you Harford seemed to me the only thing I could do!
It was because of Harford that I did what I did, and handing
it over to you seemed the only way to try and show you just

how sorry I am that I behaved as I did! It was shameful and despicable and dishonest, and you didn't deserve it!'

He was looking at her. 'And you did—you *did* deserve it? Is that what you're telling me?'

There was something in his voice that told her he was keeping himself on a very tight leash. Then he shook his head, giving a short, rasping sound in his throat.

'God Almighty, Flavia—why didn't you just tell *me*?' The question burst from him, tearing into his throat.

She could only go on staring, open mouthed. 'Tell you what?'

He swore—she couldn't understand the words, only hear the angry emotion.

'Tell me just why you got back in touch with me after you'd left London! Tell me how your father was threatening to foreclose on you and sending over an estate agent to scare you! Tell me—' his voice shook '—that you'd been nursing your grandmother, and how frail she was, and how you got called back from Palma because she was near death! *That's* what you didn't tell me—and I don't know why the *hell* you didn't!'

He took a sharp, biting breath. 'And I don't know why in *hell* you thought you had to gift me your home because you felt you *owed* it to me!'

She forced herself to her feet, forced her mouth to open. Forced herself to tell him. Spell it out for him.

'Leon, I deliberately and calculatingly started an affair with you because I wanted to save Harford. Nothing can make that not true! *Why* I had to save Harford doesn't matter! How can it? I used…sex—' she stumbled over the word but made herself say it anyway '—to stop my father foreclosing on that nightmare loan he'd made to my grandmother, which he was using to make me do what he wanted: use *sex* to keep you sweet, just as you accused me of doing! He wanted the rescue package from you. He didn't want anything jeopardising it—so if you wanted me in your bed, my God, he'd see to it that it happened!'

Her face worked but she made herself go on. Forced herself.

'I told myself I didn't have a choice! That I *had* to do what he wanted because I knew how devastated and distressed my grandmother would be, in her frail mental condition, if she had to leave Harford. So I got back in touch with you and let you take me out on dates—let you…let you take me to bed! And I knew it was wrong—knew my father was pimping me out to you—but I went along with it! I used sex to get what I wanted!' Her voice rasped bitterly. 'And to think I used to despise Anita for doing that—I was doing exactly the same thing!'

He was looking at her strangely. 'That's what you think, is it? That you're as bad as Anita?'

'*Yes*! How could I be any different from her?'

'How about,' he said tautly, 'because your motivations were somewhat different from hers? You wanted to save your home and you didn't want your grandmother to lose hers! The home your own father had saddled with iniquitous debt just so that he could blackmail you into doing what he wanted!'

He stopped, his eyes resting on her. Implacable. Drilling into her. Giving her nowhere to hide.

'And there's another difference between you, isn't there? *Isn't there*, Flavia? Don't try and deny it to me! Don't try and pretend to me that what we had together from that first night, our whole time on Santera, was only because you wanted to save your home!'

She closed her eyes in anguish, unable to bear that merciless gaze drilling into her.

'That made it *worse*,' she whispered. 'Agonisingly worse! To be so blissfully happy with you and yet to know that I was with you only in order to save Harford! I felt so guilty about it—but I couldn't tell you. How could I? Because I wasn't brave enough! I couldn't bear to have you look at me and know what I'd done, what I'd stooped to! And it wasn't only you I felt guilty about.'

Her voice dropped even more, became even more strained.

'I felt so guilty about my grandmother! There I was, so blissfully happy with you on Santera. I'd just abandoned my grandmother! When I got that phone call from her carer, telling me she'd had a sudden deterioration and was sinking fast, it was like a knife in my heart! While I was with you my grandmother had given up the last of her will to live—I'd abandoned her when she was at her weakest! I was with you and my grandmother was dying! If I had stayed at home with her she might never have deteriorated like that—'

Her eyes flew open. 'Guilt—guilt—guilt! It's all I could feel! About you, about my grandmother—however I twisted and turned. Guilt, guilt, *guilt*!' She gave a long, exhausted sigh. 'When you arrived at Harford the day of her funeral, and threw in my face what my father had said to you, I couldn't defend myself. I was exactly what you said I was. And there was no way out of it. No way.'

She inhaled heavily, lifting her head to look at him. 'Except to try and make amends to you in the way I did. It had been trying to save Harford that had made me do what I did. So giving you Harford was the only way I could try and clear up the mess I'd made—salve my conscience. Absolve me from the guilt I felt.'

She fell silent, just staring at him. Drained. He went on standing, just looking at her.

'Guilt,' he said. 'That's a word you use so much. But I am amazed...' He paused, then continued. 'Amazed you even know what the word is. His eyes were resting on her, completely unreadable. 'It's a word that seems totally and completely unknown to your father!'

His eyes flashed suddenly, and Flavia felt herself reel at the fury in them.

'My God, I always knew the man was unscrupulous—his business dealings showed me that! But to do what he did to his own daughter! And then—' his voice twisted in disgust '—to prate to me and pretend he *doted* on you!'

She gave a painful shrug. 'It was part of the act he always

put on when he got me to go up to London—he'd lent me money for a hip operation for my grandmother, and in return I had to go and stay with him sometimes, act as his hostess and all that. I hated it!'

'That's why you were so hostile and prickly all the time?'

She nodded. 'Yes.'

'Especially to me?'

'Yes.'

'Because your father had made it clear you were supposed to be "nice" to me?'

'Yes.'

She was answering monosyllabically because it was all she could do. She could feel the tension ratcheting up in her. Feel his dark eyes resting on her. Unreadable—so unreadable. She wanted out of here. There was no purpose now—none at all—in being here any longer. She'd said everything to him— confessed everything to him. He was free to go now—*surely* he was free to go? There was nothing more to confess.

Nothing more?

She felt the accusation swirling inside her—whispering, dangerous.

Liar...

No! There was nothing more she was going to confess to him! Dear God, she'd laid bare *everything*—the sordid truth of her relationship with her father, what he had got her to do and how he'd got her to do it. Told him about how twisted up she'd felt about her grandmother—about the time she'd spent with him on Santera! There was nothing else to confess to him—*nothing*!

But still that voice inside her whispered—*liar...*

He was speaking again, the words brushing like acid against her defenceless flesh.

'And so had it not been for your father's manipulation of you—had it not been for your concern over your grand-mother—you'd never have had an affair with me? Even if your grandmother hadn't been old and frail and dependent on you, you'd never had had an affair with me? Would never have had anything to do with me? Would have been totally indifferent to me.'

'Yes.'

'Liar.'

Who had said the word? Him or her? She stared at him.

'Liar,' Leon said again softly. 'If you had met me with no connection to your father, and if you had had no responsibilities towards your grandmother, what would you have done?'

His voice was changing, sending ripples of electricity trickling along the endings of her nerves. She could feel her pulse beating—insistent, strong.

'I'll tell you what you would have done, Flavia.'

He stepped towards her, cupped his hands around her face. She could feel her skin flush with heat.

'This,' he said.

His kiss was soft. As soft as velvet. His lips caressed hers and she could feel her limbs dissolve, feel her heart leap. Her mouth opened to his, her arms wound around him, clinging and clinging and clinging to his strong, hard body.

Oh, dear God, it was bliss—bliss to have him kiss her again. Leon—her own Leon—the way he had before—the way he was doing now.

He tore his mouth away, his fingertips pressing into her skull, holding her, gazing down at her. His eyes were lambent.

'This is the truth, Flavia! This is what you could never deny—and this is what absolves you! Just as the fact that you did what you did *not* for yourself but out of love and care for your grandmother! You couldn't hide the truth about this— what there is between us—whatever the foul machinations of your father, whatever your sense of guilt about yourself! When you left me, and when your father had fed me his poison about you, it gutted me to think that the time we'd had together had been based on nothing more than an attempt to use my desire for you for your own venal ends! I saw you then as what I'd feared you were when I first met you—a pampered,

idle female who was happy to live off her father's wealth. On Santera I thought I'd got that completely wrong—because you truly seemed happy in such a simple place, happy only to be with me! Then afterwards I thought *that* was the lie—and it gutted me! Gutted me because I'd thought—'

His voice choked suddenly, and Flavia could feel her arms tightening around him instinctively, protectively.

'I'd thought you were feeling about me what I had come to feel about you.' His gaze, dark and glowing, poured into her. 'But that time on Santera was true—wasn't it? *Wasn't it*? That was the true time between us—away from your father's machinations, away from your concerns about your grandmother—just you and me together. Happy. *Blissful.*' He used the word she'd used fondly, smilingly.

Lovingly.

That was what she could see in his face now. Impossible to deny—impossible to hide.

As impossible for him to hide it as it was for her…

'I made such a mess of things,' she whispered.

He shook his head. 'It was an impossible situation.' He took a heaving breath. 'I only wish that you had told me on Santera about what your father was truly like, about how you were the carer for your grandmother, about the way he was holding that debt over your head—I just wish you had told me all that.'

'I didn't dare to. I was scared you might be so angry you would call off the deal with my father, and then in revenge at my spoiling things for him he'd foreclose on that debt anyway! And my grandmother would still have lost Harford! So I didn't dare tell you—I didn't dare!' She took a shaking breath. 'And I didn't *want* to tell you—didn't want you looking at me knowing I'd let my father pimp me out to you.'

He shook her—gently but angrily. 'You did it for your grandmother! Did you think I would condemn you for that?'

'I was scared you might! And I didn't want to lose what we had because…because I knew it couldn't last. I knew I had to go back to my grandmother, that I wasn't free to have a re-lationship with you. So I…I just blotted it all out, blanked it all out.'

He kissed her softly. 'Never again. You understand me, Flavia?' he said admonishingly. 'From this moment on you trust me—you trust me with everything! I can't go through again what I've been through—wanting you from the first moment I saw you, being endlessly rebuffed by you, then you bolting from me and leaving London the way you did, having to tread on eggshells to win you, and then—dear God—losing you again after Santera and all the hell that came afterwards. Missing you, mistrusting you, accusing you and hurting like hell every moment of that time!

'And then the bombshell of the title deeds of your home landing on my desk! Telling me, once I'd found out from your solicitors, not just about the ruinous debt your father held over you, but about how you'd been your grandmother's devoted carer and how recently she'd died—all that slamming into me like punches to my gut. I'd been totally, totally wrong about you, about my accusations! I set off to try and find you after you'd yet again disappeared off the map! Hell, Flavia—noth-ing but hell! Right up till today,' he said feelingly, 'when I phoned this place and finally tracked you down!'

He kissed her again. Devouringly, possessively. Wrapping her in a bear hug that enveloped her completely.

'And now I've got you!' he said. 'And I am never, *never* letting you go again! So get your things and tell your boss you're leaving. Tell her to hire as many agency staff as she needs to cover for you and send me the bill! Because I am taking you away with me *right now.*'

He straightened, holding her elbows, looking down at her. Then, abruptly, he frowned.

'You're crying,' he said. His frown deepened. 'Why are you crying?'

His answer was a convulsive sob, and Flavia threw herself into his arms again. He held her as she cried, weeping out the tears inside her, weeping out all the guilt that had racked her for so, so long. Held her and soothed her, his strong, protective palms smoothing down her back, his lips brushing her eyelids. When all the tears were shed he kissed her again gently, so gently.

'All done?' he asked, his eyes as soft as his voice.

She nodded. All she was capable of doing.

'Good,' he said. 'Let's go.'

He led her towards the door, taking her hand. She would go with him to the ends of the earth now, and never leave him again.

Gratitude, wonder—love—filled her like light pouring through a window.

'Where to?' she asked, gazing lovingly up at him.

He smiled down at her. 'Where do you think?' He paused to kiss her nose. 'I've recently become the extremely satisfied owner of an exceptionally beautifully country house.' He paused again, this time to brush her lips with his. 'I think you'll like it,' he said. 'It's a place filled with love—a place where a beautiful, brave girl once lived. She did the wrong thing for the right reason and then found it was the right thing after all. And as her reward—' he smiled '—she got to live there happily ever after...'

He gazed into her eyes. 'Does that sound good?' he asked.

She lifted her mouth to his.

'Blissful,' she whispered. 'Because it comes with the one thing I want more than anything in the whole world—the one thing I can't live without.' She kissed him softly, with all the love in the world in it. 'You,' she said.

EPILOGUE

'How would you feel,' Leon said, with a slightly tentative questioning note in his voice, his arm around Flavia's shoulder as they stood on the terrace at Harford in the autumnal air, 'about having a helipad here? It would mean I could commute to the City and so spend more time here.'

Flavia leant into his shoulder and smiled warmly up at him. 'It's a brilliant idea. The lawn really isn't a good place to land.'

He gave a rueful laugh. 'No, I can see that. Not good for your herbaceous borders.'

It was Flavia's turn to sound tentatively questioning. 'Are you sure you want to be based here, Leon? You're not used to country living...'

'Cities are overrated,' he said dryly. 'Even now that I can live in penthouses and not on the streets. But even though I would love to be based here at Harford, there will still be more times than I would like that I have to travel abroad. Especially when I'm checking up on my South American *pro bono* projects.'

Her eyes warmed. 'Will you let me come with you?' she asked. 'I'll learn Spanish, I promise, so I won't be a total waste of space! I'd love to see all the good work you are doing.'

'I would love to show it to you. My endless concern is how few the projects are, compared with the need for them.

So many lives need to be transformed to lift people out of poverty.'

She heard the frustration in his voice and kissed him softly on the cheek. 'You're a good man, Leon Maranz. A better man than so many who have made it in this world. Think of men like my father, who's used people all his life for his own selfish ends, caring for no one but himself!'

Anger was etched into her voice. Leon looked down at her.

'Maybe there is a cosmic karma after all. His Far Eastern bail out came to nothing, and after I'd made it crystal clear to him my offer was off the table because of the way he's treated you and your mother's family he lost everything. Including the lovely Anita, who wanted a more solvent protector.'

Leon's voice changed from harsh to reassuring. 'But you needn't be afraid that he'll try and contact you. I've done a deal with him. While he leaves you totally alone and stays out of the country I'll pay him a modest monthly pension. He's taken himself off to Spain, and the last I heard he was trying to set himself up as a property developer. Don't worry,' he said caustically, 'I've got someone keeping tabs on him, and if his business ethics veer towards the dodgy I'll be leaning on him painfully. He won't intrude into your life any more.' He paused. '*Our* lives,' he amended.

He turned her towards him, gazing down at her uplifted face. Flavia felt her heart squeeze and melt with love, as she was bathed in the love-light in his dark, expressive eyes.

'Our lives, my beautiful, adored Flavia. Our lives together from now onwards. Never to be parted again.'

Softly he lowered his mouth to hers, kissing her gently with sweet, possessing passion. He cupped her face with this hands.

'I wish I could have met your grandparents to tell them how wonderful a granddaughter they raised. To tell them how grateful—how profoundly and eternally grateful I am to have found you. And to tell them—' he glanced around at the autumn splendour, framing the house in a blaze of colour

'—how beautiful their house is. How wonderful a home it will continue to be for you and me—'

'And for our children?' There was a wistful note in Flavia's voice.

He gave a warm laugh. 'Oh, yes, for our children. Definitely, *definitely* for our children. You were happy here when you were a child, and you know all the secret places in the house and in the grounds. Our children can roam wild here, be happy and carefree. And you and I—' he kissed the tip of her nose, sliding his arm around her shoulder and strolling with her towards the open French windows leading into the drawing room '—will watch them grow well and strong, and safe and loved. All our days. All our years together.'

At the entrance to the drawing room he paused and looked out over the lawns. 'We'll make a happy home. A happy family.' He drew her fast against his heart. 'A blissful, perfect marriage. Wouldn't you agree, Mrs Maranz?'

She clutched him close, radiant with happiness. 'Absolutely,' she breathed.

He laughed, happiness in his voice as in his heart. 'Then let's crack open that waiting bottle of champagne and drink to our marriage! And then...'

The expression in his eyes altered and Flavia felt a quickening of her pulse, a breathlessness in her lungs.

'And then, my beautiful, beautiful bride, I'm going to carry you upstairs and remove you from that exquisite but really quite unnecessary bridal gown you look so breathtaking in. We shall have a wedding night that will melt the very stars in heaven!'

She frowned. 'I don't think stars can melt, can they?' she queried.

'Whatever,' he said airily, and hefted the champagne bottle out of its ice-bucket. Then he paused. 'On second thought...'

He scooped up two flutes, hooked his fingers around the neck of the champagne bottle, and then, with effortless strength, scooped up Flavia as well. She cried out in laughing surprise and he grinned down at her.

'The champagne can come with us,' he said.

'Whatever,' she answered airily.

He grinned again, kissed her nose, and carried her and the champagne upstairs.

* * * * *

The World of Mills & Boon®

There's a Mills & Boon® series that's perfect for you. We publish ten series and with new titles every month, you never have to wait long for your favourite to come along.

Blaze.   Scorching hot, sexy reads

By Request   Relive the romance with the best of the best

Cherish™   Romance to melt the heart every time

Desire™   Passionate and dramatic love stories

Have Your Say

You've just finished your book.
So what did you think?

We'd love to hear your thoughts on our
'Have your say' online panel
www.millsandboon.co.uk/haveyoursay

- 🌹 Easy to use
- 🌹 Short questionnaire
- 🌹 Chance to win Mills & Boon® goodies

Visit us Online

Tell us what you thought of this book now at
www.millsandboon.co.uk/haveyoursay

YOUR_SAY